Why so much fear of tear? Because the masks we use are made of salt. A stinging, red salt which makes us beautiful and majestic but devours our skin.
Luisa Valenzuela

OTHER TITLES IN THE *MASKS* SERIES

Neil Bartlett   *Who Was That Man?*

Michael Bracewell   *The Crypto-Amnesia Club*

Ian Breakwell   *The Artist's Dream*

Leslie Dick   *Without Falling*

Janice Eidus   *Faithful Rebecca*

Alison Fell (ed.)   *The Seven Deadly Sins*

Juan Goytisolo   *Landscapes After the Battle*

Juan Goytisolo   *Marks of Identity*

Steve Katz   *Florry of Washington Heights*

Raul Nuñez   *The Lonely Hearts Club*

Luisa Valenzuela   *The Lizard's Tail*

THE
LONELY HEARTS CLUB

THE
LONELY HEARTS CLUB

RAUL NUÑEZ

Translated by Ed Emery

SERPENT'S
TAIL

The publishers thank Kathy Acker, Mark Ainley, Martin Chalmers, Bob Lumley, Enrico Palandri, Kate Pullinger, Antonio Sanchez for their advice and assistance.

British Library Cataloguing in Publication Data
Núñez, Raúl, *1946*–
 The Lonely Hearts Club
 I. Title   II. Sinatra. *English*
 863[F]
 ISBN 1-85242-137-1

First published 1989 by
Serpent's Tail, Unit 4, Blackstock Mews, London N4

Typeset by Theatretexts, London

Printed in Great Britain by
WBC Print (Bristol) Ltd.

To the Bar Paricio

Antonio bore a striking resemblance to Frank Sinatra. Forty years of age and of medium height, he was balding slightly and kept his hair close-trimmed. He'd found himself a live-in job as a night porter in a small hotel. This gave him free lodging, and a bit of money besides. About a year previously, his wife had left him to go off with a black man. Not his idea of a joke! Every time he thought of it, a wry smile appeared on his lips — the same wry smile with which he confronted the world at large. Now he no longer had a wife. It pained him when he thought of it. He felt alone in the world.

Antonio, or Frankie as he was known, used to spend his nights listening to the radio. Night-time programmes dedicated to people like himself. He liked music. One night he'd rung in to the radio station to ask them to play a Sinatra record. He didn't say anything about his nickname, or the fact that he looked like the singer. The DJ was happy to oblige. Frankie lit a cigarette and listened. He spoke no English, but he understood every word. He remembered his wife. And the black man. And once again he smiled.

Frankie had always wanted to have a kid. He didn't know why. In fact he found it strange. His wife was only twenty years old, and didn't fancy the hassle. She used to say that there was plenty of time for all that. Frankie thought otherwise. He'd met her in a bar where she worked as a waitress. The first thing that she'd said to him was that he looked like Frank Sinatra. And that was the start of it all.

They got married.

At that time, Frankie was a door-to-door salesman for a cosmetics company. He didn't earn a lot, but on the other hand the job wasn't unpleasant. He was surprised at how easy it was to sweet-talk housewives with a little smile. Women used to invite him in for coffee so that they could tell him about their problems. And on more than one occasion he came within an ace of being dragged off to bed by one of his customers.

Frankie would get home just as his wife was leaving for the bar. He'd prepare himself a bite to eat, switch on the telly and pour himself a drink. At midnight he'd go to bed, and that was his life.

His wife had Sundays off, which meant that they could spend all day together. And that was fine. They had time to make love, cook a meal and go to the pictures. Frankie wasn't unduly worried by his wife's job. He knew that it only involved sitting with the customers, holding their hands, and getting them as drunk as possible in the shortest possible time. For the first time in his life he felt contented. That is, until the black man appeared and his wife disappeared.

Frankie jacked in his job, and locked himself in the flat for a week. He divided his time between drinking, cursing and crying. One morning he woke up vomiting cognac. He'd soaked the sheets with a dark-coloured sticky liquid. He got up, went to the bathroom, had a shower, shaved and went out into the street. He decided that he wasn't going to return to the little flat where he'd lived with his wife, and went off instead to a cheap hotel in Calle Hospital. A few days later they offered him a job as night-porter, and Frankie accepted.

His job involved spending his nights sitting behind a desk next to a board full of keys, waiting for people to ring at the door. When a new guest arrived, he would make them welcome and hand them a key. If somebody had to pay, he'd note the amount in a book and keep the money in a cash box. This was the sum of his duties. Sometimes he'd end up talking with the people who were staying in the hotel, but not for long if he could help it. His main concern was getting through the night. He'd make himself a coffee every now and then, smoke a few cigarettes, and listen to the radio or read a magazine.

In the mornings he'd sleep in. Occasionally he had disturbing dreams, but he could never remember them afterwards. When he got up, he'd go for breakfast in the bar next to the hotel. He'd hang out there for a couple of hours, sitting on a bar-stool, watching the street go by and drinking black coffee and brandy. Then he'd take a stroll, or maybe go to the pictures, or back to his room.

Frankie knew that things weren't going right for him. In the last few days he'd had diarrhoea. An unexpected and violent attack which shook him through and through. There was no obvious reason for it. He felt healthy enough. It lasted for a while, and went away as fast as it had come. A little while later, he began to notice that his hands were beginning to shake slightly. He decided that something was wrong with him. One night an advert in a magazine caught his eye. It was an ad for a lonely hearts correspondence club. For a small sum of money, they would send him hundreds of addresses of people who were just like him. He could spend his nights writing to them, and then wait for their replies. It sounded like a good idea. He cut out the ad, filled in his name and address, stuck it in an envelope. The following day he posted it. This made him feel a bit better.

Several days later, Frankie received a plain brown envelope through the post. He stuck it in his jacket pocket and didn't open it until the evening. It was a brochure, with photographs of people. Passport-size pictures of lonely people. There they all were. One next to the other. If he decided to join the club, he would become one of them, and his photograph would join the others in the brochure. He took a closer look at their faces.

There were all sorts. People who wanted to talk about their problems. People trying to find themselves a partner. People who needed love. People who might otherwise have thrown themselves from a bridge or stuck their heads in the oven. The kind of people that you meet in deserted bars on Sunday afternoons. People who were neat and shaved. People with long hair and wild looks. People who had good jobs. People who didn't have a penny. People incapable of smiling. People who slept alone. People who got drunk. People who drank only tea. People who had been abandoned. People who were taking one last gamble on life. Frankie decided to join.

A few days later, he received, together with his first list of addresses, his first letter — a small blue envelope, written in a delicate hand. Frankie took a long look at it without daring to open it. He read the sender's name. It was a woman. He'd had no contact with women since his wife had left him. He used to just watch them, as if they were something remote and unattainable. There was only one time — when he'd been in a bar on Calle Robador. It was a Sunday evening when he had nothing else to do. He felt a physical need for someone to touch him. There were five or six women in the bar, leaning up against the juke box or sitting on stools. Frankie had a bit of money in his pocket. He went up to one of them. She was very young, with long dyed-blonde hair. Her face seemed frozen in a permanent smile. Frankie felt a moment of fear. For a full year his only sex had been masturbation. They went to a room upstairs.

"We'll have to get a move on," she said. "My husband's waiting for me downstairs."

Frankie sat on the bed, and felt decidedly ill.

"Well?" said the girl. "Are we going to do it, or not?"

"Not, I suppose."

"Well, it's up to you. Are you going to pay me?"

"Of course."

And that was that.

He took another look at the blue envelope. For a moment he thought of packing it in and finishing with the club. It wouldn't have taken much for him to do precisely that. He decided to go down to the bar for a beer. He ended up drinking half a dozen. When he'd ordered up his seventh, he opened the letter and read:

Dear Mr Castro,

I saw your photograph in the brochure that the club sends out, and I was surprised how much you look like the singer Frank Sinatra. For a moment I thought that it had been a mistake, or maybe a joke on the part of the club, although then I realized that you're a lot younger than him. I suppose you must be tired of everybody telling you this, but I felt bound to say it.

If you'll allow me, I'll tell you a few things about myself.

I am forty-five years old, and have been a widow for the last ten years. My life is very simple, and a bit unhappy. The only thing that gives me the strength to carry on is my son, who is eighteen years of age, but he also gives me a lot of problems, which would be a bit complicated to go into. I also have a cat called Bolita, which I love very much. I work in the offices of a major company, and I have a lot of male colleagues, but I've never made any close relationships there. Sometimes I find it hard to get friendly with people, and that was why I decided to join the club. When I leave work, I feel as if I am lost. When I get home, I turn on the TV and I leave it on till the epilogue, although I don't always watch it. As for my son, I see him very little,

because he doesn't enjoy staying at home, and he
spends his days on the streets with his friends. For some
time now I've had problems sleeping. I spend the night
tossing around in bed and thinking all sorts of silly
things. Several times I've ended up having to go to work
without having slept a wink all night. I've been to see
a doctor about it, but he says that there's nothing wrong
with me.

I feel that something's missing from my life.

I would be very happy if you would tell me
something about your own life, because judging by your
photograph, you must be a sensitive and good-natured
person. Maybe you'll find me not very interesting, but
I hope that we'll get to know each other a bit better,
and that we will end up being friends.

Yours sincerely,
Hortensia Garcia,
widow of Conejero
PS: I enclose a photograph of myself.

Frankie studied the woman's photograph. She wasn't
particularly striking. An older woman, with dark hair and
a round face. Nothing special about her. Not somebody he
knew. He'd never seen her before in his life, but there she
was, in black and white. He felt confused, and noticed a
queasy feeling in his guts. Too many beers. He went to
the toilet and threw up. This made him feel better, so he
took a double coffee and read the letter through again.

He was at a loss what to do.

That night he found himself thinking of his wife again.
In some ways he had been hoping that somebody younger
would write to him, but maybe things weren't that easy.
Still, he could always hope. There were hundreds of nights
ahead, and the letters would keep coming.

Frankie looked at his watch. It was 3.05 in the morning.
It would be just his luck for somebody to turn up looking

for a room now. He fancied a little nap in his chair.

He cast his eye up and down the long, narrow hotel corridor with its faded notices, handwritten in biro.

Residents Are Requested Not To Make a Noise.

Visitors Are Not Allowed in Guests' Rooms.

Down each side of the corridor there were a dozen or so doors, each painted dark-brown and numbered. And behind those doors were people trying to get a night's rest. Some were plainly not succeeding. Frankie could hear their coughing, their little noises in the night. He could see the pathetic little 30-watt lightbulbs lighting up in the dark and then flicking off again. He could see them as they got up to go for a piss. They moved slowly and silently, like ghosts, as they returned to their rooms. And sometimes they would come out again to ask him for a cigarette, to discuss the weather, anything, so as not to go crazy. Some of the men needed a woman, or maybe had lost the woman in their lives. Others needed a job of some sort. As for the women, they were all missing a husband or a son. And all of them lacked a home. Frankie knew them inside-out. He knew the ageing crazies who spent their nights in conversation with their canaries. He knew the small-time criminals who sold drugs on the Plaza Real. He knew the lonely kitchen hands who spent their time masturbating over cheap porno magazines. He knew the sinister Moroccans who went out thieving in the night. He knew the police who came looking for them. He knew the ones who had gone mad in their rooms. He also knew those who had survived. He knew them all.

All of a sudden he felt the urge to reply to the letter that he'd received.

He imagined the woman in a simple, tidy room, alone in her double bed, her head resting on a white pillow, her cat sleeping at her feet.

Who knows, perhaps she was thinking of him.

At that moment, he would have liked to be with her,

doing a crossword, playing backgammon or drinking a cup of coffee. She wasn't much to look at, but who cares.

Frankie remembered that there was a whole bottle of cheap cognac in the hotel's little kitchen. He knew the alcohol wasn't going to agree with him, but he couldn't resist. He got up, went to the kitchen, fetched the bottle and a glass and poured himself a generous helping. The brandy smelt vile. For a moment he thought he might have picked up a bottle of paraffin by mistake. Despite the smell, it improved his frame of mind. He turned on the radio. Not too loud. A female announcer with a velvety voice was talking, just to him. He went and sat down, tipped his chair back and stuck his feet on the edge of the table. He gave his undivided attention to the brandy for a good half-hour, and finally took pen and paper and began to write.

Dear Senora Garcia,
I'm as drunk as a rat. I'm seeing double, and I think I'm going to fall off my chair. You probably think that I'm just an alcoholic, but if I hadn't had a drink, I probably wouldn't have written to you. I've become frightened of women. A little while ago I was thinking that you were probably alone in your bed, and I would have liked to have been there with you. Please don't get me wrong. I only mean so that we could play cards together or something like that. I'm sure you'll never write to me again, because this paper must stink of brandy. But there you go...

If I had pots of money and plenty of women, I wouldn't have needed to join the club. This week I sent off a pools coupon, but I doubt that I'll win anything. We'll see.

I've always been a clean-living sort of person, and I've earned my living selling shampoo and face-creams door to door. I used to have friends and a girl or two I'd go out with. Then I got married, and within a year my wife went and left me.

These days I'm working as a night porter in a hotel.
I'm in a terrible state. I feel like a witch has put a spell
on me. I smile at kids and they run a mile. You'll have
to forgive me, Senora Garcia, I'm going to pour myself
another drink.

Here's to us!

So, what would you think about inviting me to dinner
at your house? Who knows, we might get on together.
Let's give it a go... My favourite food is stewed veal,
and I bet you're a heavenly cook.

I suppose I must be talking a lot of rubbish, but my
head's buzzing. I'm drunk. Any minute now, someone's
going to turn up wanting a room. Just what I need! I'll
tell him I've lost the keys, and I'll send him to sleep on
a bench on the Ramblas.

I have problems with my socks, Hortensia, because
I never learnt to sew, and every time I get a hole in a
sock I have to go and buy a new pair. It's costing me a
fortune. Do you think I was right to put down
Salamanca-Betis as an away win?
Yours sincerely,
Frank Sinatra.

Frankie put the letter in an envelope, wrote the address,
stuck a stamp on, and polished off the brandy in his glass.
For several minutes he left the hotel to its own devices
and staggered down the ill-lit pavement of Calle Hospital.
He popped the letter into the box on San Agustin, and then
returned to his desk.

2

F rankie woke up to find his trousers wrapped round his head like a turban. His efforts to get into bed had failed and he'd ended up sleeping on the floor. One of his shoes had wound up on top of the wardrobe, and the other was still on his foot. He felt like an elephant was stamping on his head, and his stomach felt like it was being burned up by white phosphorus.

He opened his eyes cautiously, got up slowly, and went over to the small washbasin in the corner of the room. He drank three glasses of water and splashed his face. He was beginning to feel better. He lit a cigarette, stretched out on the bed and tried to remember. He had a notion that he'd done something terrible — that he had written a letter to a woman or maybe murdered somebody. He wasn't sure of anything. All he could summon up were confused images involving a bottle of cheap brandy and wandering around in Calle Hospital.

At that moment somebody knocked at the door.

"Hey, Frankie... You in?"

"Yes. What's up?"

"It's me, Manolo."

Manolo was fifty if he was a day. He was in charge of the hotel during the day. He was a small, lascivious Galician, hairy as an ape, who spent all his money on special ointments for keeping up erections, custom condoms and similar items that he never had the opportunity to use.

"What is it, Manolo?"

"There's a letter for you."

Frankie gave a little shudder.

"A letter... ? For me?"

"That's right. Shall I bring it?"

"No, wait. I'll be out to get it. I was just coming."

"As you like."

Frankie heard Manolo's footsteps receding down the long corridor. For a moment he lay there without moving. Then he began to dress. His hands had started shaking again. He told himself he needed a beer. Just one.

He found the letter on the desk where he passed his nights. He saw it straight away. At one glance he read his name on the envelope, which this time was not blue, but pink. He picked it up and rushed out into the street.

He meant to go into his local bar, but by mistake he went into the tobacconist's next door.

He asked for a beer, and the woman behind the counter gave him a strange look.

"I'm sorry, sir, but we don't sell beer," she stuttered.

Frankie looked around as if searching for a table, gave a nervous laugh, passed his hand across his forehead, bought a packet of Ducados, paid with a hundred-peseta note and fled without waiting for the change. He was nervous; he had another unknown woman in his pocket.

He found himself in the middle of the Ramblas, with a mighty hangover and a strong feeling of panic.

Nowhere to go. He walked from Canaletas down to the port, and then, tired and thirsty, he went into a bar for a beer.

With the tip of his finger, he caressed the letter lightly, but only for a moment, because it felt like it had given him an electric shock.

As he sat at the bar counter, he thought about this new woman.

He wondered what colour knickers she wore, how many

boyfriends she'd had, what she was expecting from him, what sort of noise she made as she was sleeping on winter nights, how much money it would take to buy her, and what kind of heaven or hell he was going to find at her side.

He still couldn't bring himself to open the letter.

He remembered one night when his wife had come back a bit tired from her job at the bar and had woken him up.

"Frankie, you're going to have to help me."

He had got up, half-undressed, brought over his rep's case and pretended that she was a customer and he was trying to sell her some anti-wrinkle cream. She had laughed and laughed, throwing her head back and shaking her hair. All night long they'd played at buying and selling, until she finally fell asleep.

This not particularly significant incident had been brought to mind by the sight of a girl who'd come into the bar and sat down almost next to him. He gave her a long, hard look.

She was no more than a kid. Her hair was short and almond-coloured, with a fringe. She was wearing a white Snoopy sports-shirt and a pair of jeans. She could have had the most beautiful face in the world, but she was cross-eyed! She was carrying a baby in her arms, wrapped in a blanket.

All of a sudden Frankie tensed up. He felt afraid again. He tried to tell himself she was just a harmless kid who'd sat down next to him and ordered a coffee. But it didn't help. He started getting twinges in his legs. He burped.

Suddenly she turned and asked him for a cigarette.

Frankie was completely lost for words. He had his packet of Ducados on the table, but the problem was that he didn't know which eye to look at. Her baby appeared to be asleep.

"Help yourself," he said.

His words came out smooth as honey. As if it hadn't been him speaking, but the real Sinatra. She smiled, stretched out a hand and took one of his Ducados. Holding it between two fingers, she asked:

"Have you got a light?"

Frankie searched for a non-existent lighter, and had obviously forgotten about the box of matches that he'd been twiddling between his fingers.

"No, sorry," he answered.

"What's that, then?"

The girl gestured to his matchbox with the end of her nose.

"Oh, I'm sorry!" he exclaimed, and he lit the cigarette for her.

For several long minutes they didn't say anything. Frankie was thinking about the girl's eyes and the way they crossed each other like two swords fighting a duel.

"Something getting you down?" she asked.

Frankie decided to look her in the left eye. At the same time, his eyes wandered down to her breasts, which stood out like two gumboils on Snoopy's cheeks.

"Well, you know, everyone's got problems..."

She nodded agreement and looked sadly at her baby.

"I'm not doing too well myself."

"The kid, you mean?"

"Both of us."

Frankie gave way to a moment of boldness.

"I'd like to help you," he declared.

The girl shook her head.

"Thanks, but I don't think you can."

"Well at least you could tell me what you need," Frankie urged her. "After all, just now you were offering to help me."

"It's not easy to explain, you see. I've only known you a few minutes."

"Can I ask what your name is?" Frankie ventured.

She shrugged her shoulders and smiled again.

"I've got a very plain name," she answered. "I don't think I'm going to tell you."

"Well people must call you something."

"Yes, they call me Natalia. But that's not my real name, you know. And his name's David," she added, pointing to the baby.

"And my name's Frankie... I mean Antonio."

"That's a good name," said Natalia, with a childish grimace.

A rare feeling of tranquillity was creeping up on Frankie. For years he couldn't remember having talked with a young woman like this, except when he went to the baker's, or went to his usual shop to buy a pair of socks. He took a sip of beer and told himself that life was looking up. The pink envelope was no longer ticking like a time-bomb in his pocket.

"I've left home, you know," she suddenly confided.

The glass trembled almost imperceptibly in Frankie's hand, and once again the wry smile returned to his lips.

"Who have you left, your husband or your folks?" he asked.

"All of them."

"And have you got... I mean, do you know anyone who can help you... or get you somewhere to live?"

"No, nobody. I'd like to find a room in a boarding house somewhere, but I'm under-age and I haven't got any money."

"A boarding house?"

"Yes. Something like that."

"How old are you, Natalia?"

"Sixteen."

Frankie finished off the rest of his beer, felt another twinge of panic, and then plucked up courage and said:

"I work as a night porter in a small hotel. Maybe I could do something."

He saw two little shooting stars in Natalia's eyes. She

said nothing. She looked at her baby, and after a long pause asked:

"Will I have to go to bed with you, Antonio?"

Frankie couldn't help himself. He ran his hand through Natalia's hair like she was a puppy, gave her nose a little tweak, and said:

"Of course, kid. Not only with me, but with everyone in the hotel. And with the drunks from the bar on the corner. And with the old woman who sells raffle tickets for the blind. And with the man who comes to take away the gas bottles. And with the man who comes to read the electric meter. But most of all with me. At least a dozen times a day."

Natalia began to laugh.

"I think you're crazy, Antonio. Much crazier than me!"

"Sure. I don't know how I'm going to manage to get you into the hotel, though."

"I don't want to cause you problems, Antonio. Forget it. I'll manage somehow."

"Leave it up to me. I think I can fix something," said Frankie, lost in thought.

Natalia took a fifty-peseta piece out of her little purse.

"It's all I've got. Would you like to share a beer with me?"

All of a sudden, without waiting for an answer, Natalia started laughing again. But this time her laugh was somehow weird and distant. She showed her teeth and stretched her lips for something that didn't exist. As if her laugh was for some apparition hidden behind the bar. Frankie knew that it wasn't for him. Natalia laughed for several minutes. The baby was still asleep.

"Shall we go?" Frankie suggested.

When they reached the hotel, they could see Manolo sitting at the desk, next to the board with the keys on it, completely absorbed in trying to solve a Rubik's cube which he was turning between his fingers.

"How goes, Manolo?" said Frankie, by way of greeting.

"It's a pig," replied the Galician, without so much as looking up. "You know how to do these things?"

"No idea."

"I'll show you, if you like. You've no idea how hard..."

"Listen, Manolo."

"What?"

"I need to talk to you."

"Now?"

"Yes. Now."

Manolo looked slightly irritated, put aside his Rubik's cube and for the first time noticed Natalia. She responded with a child-like smile.

"Hi, Manolo," she said, simply.

"Hi..."

Frankie went over to him, took him by the arm and led him down the corridor, leaving Natalia and her baby in a rickety old armchair, the only one that the hotel possessed.

"Listen, Manolo, I'm going to have to ask you a favour. But before I do, I must tell you that I'm not going to touch the girl, and neither are you. OK?"

"Look pal, I..."

"OK. All I want to do is get her a room without her having to pay for it. I met her in a bar. She's under-age, she's left home, she's got a baby, and she hasn't got a cent. Look, you know room 24 is empty. All we have to do is put her in there and she'll be fine. What do you reckon?"

"For fuck's sake, Frankie, you're always coming up with these weird ideas. What if the Lizard shows up?"

The Lizard was eighty-three years of age and the owner of the hotel. He generally turned up round about the first of the month, picked up his money, took a stroll up and down the corridor, went for a piss, and was off again. He had never been known to vary his routine.

"You know the Lizard knows nothing about anything. What's more, he was here last week, so he's not due back for at least three weeks."

"I'm worried, though, Frankie. I could end up without a job."

"Don't worry. You can always blame it on me."

"But she's just a kid... I mean, the police are likely to come looking for her and..."

"Don't you worry. I'll see to it. You've never seen her before in your life, OK?"

"OK," Manolo agreed, with an air of resignation.

Frankie went back to where Natalia was sitting, lit a cigarette, and, with a small hint of his former self-assurance, said:

"Come on, Natalia. It's all fixed."

The room was barely larger than the small bed it contained. There were no windows. The walls were decorated with various obscene graffiti. The door was riddled with little holes, that were filled with newspaper. A yellowish bulb hung from the ceiling. And that was it.

"All yours, Natalia. As you can see, it's not the Ritz, but it's the best I can do."

She looked at this hole as if it was the boudoir of an Egyptian queen.

"Oh, Antonio, it's... it's wonderful!"

She gave Frankie a quick kiss on the cheek, and promptly flung her baby up in the air. It smashed against the ceiling, bounced against the wall and ended up in a little bundle on the floor.

Frankie was paralysed for a moment.

"Jesus, Natalia, you've killed him... " he stammered.

"I'm so happy!" she shouted, laughing out loud.

It was then that Frankie got a good look at the baby. It was fucking rubber! One of those bald-headed monstrosities that are life-size reproductions of real babies.

Frankie felt his guts wrenched by a violent earthquake. It had been a long time since his diarrhoea had troubled him. Now his legs were trembling again. He turned pale.

"Sorry, Natalia, I'll be back," he muttered rapidly, and

he rushed off to the toilet.

He sat on the pan, emptied his bowels rather abruptly, and, while he was at it, pulled out the pink envelope. He opened it and began to read.

To Senor Antonio Castro:
Dear Antonio,
I am fifty-two years old and I work as a waiter in a bar in the Barrio Chino.

My real name is Rosendo, but everybody calls me Rosita, for reasons that I suppose you can guess.

I was born in Cadiz, but I've been living in Barcelona for a few years now. Everybody thinks I'm a load of laughs, because I'm always cracking jokes, and when they shut the bar I sing flamenco and sometimes I get up on the tables and dance. When I was younger I used to be on the stage, and I've kept some good photos from those days. These days, though, when I get home at night, I sometimes find myself crying. I don't want my mother to know, because the poor dear is getting on a bit, and she'd worry. I'm in love with a young man who has been working in the bar for the last three months. His name is Ramon, and he's from Andalucia just like me. He ignores me completely and all he does is take money off me. A few days ago, I bought myself a blonde wig to see if he'd like that better, but no luck. He's less appreciative than ever, and what's more he makes fun of me.

I joined the club to find someone who would truly love me, because my heart is broken and I need someone to help me. I thought of leaving my job so as to get away from Ramon, but I suppose I prefer to be in his company, even though he's ignoring me, rather than losing him forever.

It would be nice if you could come to the bar and we could have couple of drinks together. If you're not into men, that's OK, we could just be friends. I'd also love you to hear me sing *The Locket*, which is my favourite song.

Do please write.

Rosendo Lopez.

When Frankie got back to Natalia's room, he found her fast asleep on the bed, holding the rubber doll in her arms. He gently pulled the tatty blanket over her, gave her a little kiss on the forehead and quietly crept out.

3

The second letter from Hortensia Garcia reached Frankie on a Monday morning. In a way it was a relief. He felt he was dealing with a woman who was calm and sensible, and even thinking about her made him feel better. For the past few days he'd done nothing but look after Natalia, and his nerves were beginning to fray. He still knew nothing about the girl. Somewhere or other she must have a family or a home. He had to get food for her. What's more, she asked him to fetch milk for her doll, and refused to leave her room. Frankie had offered her affection, and he could hardly just abandon her. Manolo suggested that he take her to a mental hospital.

What's more, he had Rosendo Lopez, aka Rosita, on his mind. He'd had a dream about him. He'd met Rosendo in a pink forest, pouring a milky coffee for his mother and crying over his bar-room boyfriend. Frankie wanted to help him. He had meant to write to him, or to visit him, but he hadn't dared. He'd looked for his photo in the club's brochure. The man was bald, fat, and with a face like a ship's figurehead.

At that moment Natalia appeared in the hotel corridor.

"Antonio..."

"What?"

"The baby's ill. He's got a fever."

Frankie ran one hand across his brow, closed his eyes and chewed his lip.

"What do you want me to do about it, Natalia?"

"Call a doctor."

"What?!"

"Yes, you'll have to get a doctor... I think it's serious."

"We could wait for a bit, and give him an aspirin to see if it does any good," said Frankie, trying to be patient.

"No, you'll have to go straight away."

An idea flashed into Frankie's head.

"Look, Natalia, there's something I've not told you... I'd like you to know now. Listen carefully."

She stood and listened in silence.

"I was a student till a few years ago. But I had to give it up. I didn't have enough money, times were hard, and I had to go out and get a job. I was studying medicine. I only had one more year to go before I got my doctor's diploma. You can rely on me, I'll see to David."

Natalia fixed Frankie with her oblique look.

"You're not trying to trick me, are you?"

"I promise."

"All right then, come on," said Natalia. She took Frankie by the hand and hauled him off to her room.

The doll was lying on the bed, with a blanket drawn up to its chin. All you could see was its rubber head resting on the pillow.

"Poor thing," said Natalia. "He's fallen asleep..."

Frankie approached the bed, rested the palm of his hand on the doll's forehead and after a few seconds withdrew it.

"He's running a high fever, isn't he," she said, anxiously.

"It's nothing serious, Natalia. He's just caught a bit of a cold."

"You ought to examine him a bit more closely."

Frankie drew aside the blanket and, with some revulsion, put his ear to the doll's chest. For a moment he imagined that the monster's heart was actually beating. It was as if he could hear the beating of a real heart.

"This baby is fine," he said finally. "You can relax."

"Antonio, please tell me the truth."

"It's like I told you."

Natalia covered the doll with the blanket and kissed it on the forehead.

"He's all I've got, you see."

"You've got me as well, though."

"Sure, but that's different."

Frankie looked at his watch. He wanted to be on his own so as to read his new letter. He was worried that spending all this time with Natalia would send him barmy, but at the same time it pained him to walk out and leave her. He looked at her affectionately.

"I'm going to have to go, love. Don't worry though, I'll be back later to see how the baby's getting on."

Natalia sat on the bed and bowed her head.

"I'll stay here and wait for you."

"OK. See you later," said Frankie as he fled to seek refuge in his own room.

Once he was on his own again, he gave a sigh of relief, locked the door and stretched out on his bed. He took the letter and laid it next to him on the blanket. He looked at it for a minute or two. This woman was going to have to help him. Who knows, maybe she could advise him what to with Natalia, or whether he should visit Rosendo Lopez. He couldn't remember whether he'd actually replied to the woman's first letter, but he felt relaxed about it. The envelope, like the previous one, was blue, and the neatness of her handwriting somehow reassured him. What with one thing and another, he was feeling the need for a drink. It occurred to him that if he carried on with this club, he'd end up being a candidate for Alcoholics Anonymous.

"OK, chum. Anchors away...!" he thought, as he opened the letter.

Dear Antonio,

I received your letter, and first of all I want to say that I understand you perfectly, and I didn't think it was at all bad that you wrote to me after a drink or two. I admire your honesty, and I'm glad you feel that you can confide your problems to me. I know that disappointment in love is a very sad thing, but you should remember that you're not the first to suffer it, and there are many people in the world who suffer far worse things. For a long while I used to be involved in my local parish church, helping people in need, but then, for some reason, I stopped.

I hope that you're getting over your fear of women. You can trust me not to hurt you, and I may even be able to help you to get through your present bad patch.

I really enjoyed your letter, and found some bits of it very entertaining. There's one thing, though — I suppose it's none of my business, really, but you should try to stay off the alcohol, because I've seen so many people ruin their lives through drink, and I wouldn't want the same thing to happen to you.

For my part, I would be very happy to meet you in person, and so, if you think it's a good idea, I would like to invite you to lunch at my house this Sunday. I'm not such a good cook as you think, but I'll do something nice for you.

I enclose my visiting card. Why don't you phone me one evening to let me know if you can make it. I can't think of anything else to say at the moment, but we'll have plenty of time to talk on Sunday (always assuming that you want to come, of course).
With best regards,
Hortensia.

Frankie smiled a smile that lasted for several minutes. There was a lot of promise in a letter like that. A paper woman, dressed in blue letters, was inviting him round for a meal. He had become used to eating alone. He'd forgotten what it was like to sit at a table next to a woman.

Gradually, though, that old sense of unknown danger came creeping back. His smile left him. A series of appalling possibilities opened before him.

Maybe he would be sick all over Hortensia's white tablecloth. Maybe a fishbone would get stuck in his throat. Or he might burp horribly loudly. Or maybe he'd be so clumsy that he'd break all her glasses. Perhaps an olive would go flying off his fork and fix itself in her eye. Or maybe he'd be incapable of eating a thing. Or maybe, just maybe, everything would turn out well, and he'd never want to eat alone again as long as he lived.

He felt that the whole enterprise was foolhardy and ridiculous. What was he going to wear? He only had two shirts, one white and one brown. He couldn't decide between them. He looked at his shoes. They needed a good polish, and the sole of one of them was beginning to come off. He dived under the bed and found a pair of boots, but they were too scruffy to be of any use. He had three pairs of crumpled trousers that were definitely out of fashion. He went to the wardrobe, opened it, and tried to find a tie. No tie. He couldn't turn up to lunch with nothing to wear. He was going to have to buy some clothes. But he was skint. Natalia and her baby doll had been costing him a fortune. He decided to go and borrow some money from someone, but he couldn't think who.

The realization dawned that he had no friends.

Maybe the easiest way would be to borrow clothes from people in the hotel. Manolo was in the habit of wearing dayglo jackets, though. The idea didn't appeal to him. The other alternative was to chuck a bit of money into the fruit machine and go for the jackpot. Five thousand pesetas. That would do him nicely. With a couple of wins on a Lucky Player, his problem would be solved. But then he decided that this was just a pipe-dream, and he stopped thinking about it.

There was no obvious solution in sight, so he went to

sit on a stool in the bar next door to the hotel.

Right now he needed something strong. He ordered up a Cuba Libre and lit a cigarette. He glanced at the one-armed bandit in the corner and thought of giving it a whirl, but then he lost his nerve. He'd end up blowing all his money. He needed help.

Rosendo Lopez — Rosita — popped into his head as he was halfway through his second Cuba Libre. He had no idea what good it would do him, but he decided to go to see him at the bar, and put his problem to him. It was only a few streets away. For the time being this was the best he could think of. Frankie finished off his second Cuba Libre, paid his bill, and stepped confidently out into the street.

The bar was called the "Queen of Muscatel". It was located on the corner of Calle Cadena. It wasn't particularly large — just four or five tables, at one of which a bored customer was sitting, smoking a pipe. The bar's green-painted walls were covered with pictures of football teams and naked blondes. A young man with the looks of a gypsy was washing glasses behind the wooden counter. Frankie guessed that this must be Ramon.

"Excuse me," he said.

"Yes?" the young man replied, barely raising his eyes.

"I'm looking for Rosendo Lopez. I believe he works here."

"Who?"

"Rosendo Lopez."

The young man looked blank. Frankie hesitated for a moment and then added:

"I mean... Rosita."

Ramon shrugged contemptuously and carried on washing glasses.

"Today's his day off, but he'll probably call in, if you want to wait..."

"OK, I'll wait for a bit. Give me a Cuba Libre."

Frankie waited for two hours. He felt ridiculous and pathetic. Every now and then he decided to leave, but for some reason didn't. Here he was, expecting to get clothes, or money, or maybe just words of sympathy, from someone he didn't know from Adam, and who could probably spare no more than a pair of underpants anyway.

By this time he'd downed too many rums and was feeling decidedly ill. He looked at his watch, shrugged his shoulders, and then, as he raised his eyes, he saw Rosita walking into the bar.

This bizarre creature looked like an overweight vampire with copper-coloured hair. He had a thick layer of make-up on his huge moon-face. His eyebrows were two slender bleached arches over a pair of bulging eyes. His mouth looked as if it had been stained by strawberry yoghurt. He was wearing a tight-fitting twinset jacket and jeans. A white plastic handbag hung from his left arm. He was wearing a lethal perfume which inundated the bar. He moved like a fashion model showing off the latest autumn collection.

Rosita headed straight for the counter without looking over to the tables. Before Frankie could make a run for it, he turned his head for a second and their eyes met.

Rosita stepped back in surprise, paused, and then came over to Frankie's table.

"My dear boy, you've come to see me," he said, fondly, as he placed a kiss on his forehead.

Frankie was struck dumb. He couldn't say a word. He just wished that he could disappear under the table, or die.

"You don't know how happy I am to see you. I never even expected a letter from you, and here you are. Ramon, darling, pour us a couple of drinks. What do you fancy, honey?"

Frankie shrugged his shoulders and looked forlorn.

"Oh dear, I do hope there's nothing wrong with you," Rosita went on. "You're so pale. You don't feel ill, do you?"

"A bit," Frankie replied hesitantly.

Rosita looked him in the eye. She knew what the problem was. She knew what made men tick. She knew what Frankie needed, but she didn't say it. And she was scared too. She'd had this fear ever since she had discovered that her body had sexual demands of its own to make. Now Frankie was in her hands. Everything depended on her now.

"Antonio, love..."

With her index finger she gently raised Frankie's chin.

"Are you listening?"

"Yes, but I can't talk."

Rosita brought her face close to Frankie's. Somebody had put a record on the jukebox, a rhumba. Another customer came into the bar.

"Can you look me in the eye?"

Frankie found himself enveloped in the vapour of a pungent perfume with the flavour of chemical bananas. His head was beginning to spin. On another occasion he would have dived for the door. He asked himself what his wife was doing at this very moment, and why she wasn't there to help him. In his mind's eye he saw several things. He saw a desolate big wheel in a deserted amusement park. He saw the bald head of the baby doll resting against Natalia's little breasts. He saw the dark corridor of the boarding house, with its vases of dried flowers. He saw a black and white TV screen with the face of Senora Hortensia. He saw Manolo murdering the Lizard on a bed of red banknotes. He saw himself, with his face hidden behind a mask of keys.

"What you need is a joint, love. You'll see, then you'll feel like a new man," Rosita said, bringing him back to earth.

Frankie had never smoked a joint, but he agreed, nodding his head laboriously.

Rosita pulled a mirror out of her bag. She touched up

her lipstick with an ineffably feminine gesture, and smiled when she saw the look on his face. Frankie remained glued to the electric chair in the bar. Miles away.

Ramon arrived with the two rums. He didn't look at either of them. He simply put the glasses down on the table and returned to the bar.

"Do you like women, Antonio?" Rosita asked.

Frankie didn't reply. He noticed that his little finger was trembling slightly.

"Look, love," Rosita continued. "If you ask me, you're carrying a lot of pain around with you, and it's eating into your soul. That's the reason why you've come here, isn't it?"

"I miss my wife," Frankie confessed, like a child.

Rosita shook her head and took a long sip of rum.

"She's left you, eh?"

"And I'm also very fond of this girl with a squint."

"Poor boy..."

"And I'm going to Sunday dinner with a lady called Hortensia."

"Look, Antonio," said Rosita after a moment's reflection. "I think you'd be better if you stopped all this drinking, because it'll only eat away at your heart, and you'll end up wrecked. If you like, we could go to my house, relax, listen to a bit of music, and roll a joint. Then you'll see, everything will get better. OK?"

"But... what about your mum?"

"Don't worry about her. The poor thing's not all there."

"The thing is, I've got no clothes and no money."

"What do you mean, love?" Rosita asked, with a look of surprise.

"I don't know."

"Well, never mind, we'll get you sorted out and then you can tell me everything."

Frankie didn't answer.

"And I want to talk to you too. About Ramon," added

Rosita, in a low voice.

"OK. Let's go."

Rosita lived in an dingy three-storey building in a street close to the bar. The dilapidated main door was made of wood. It opened onto a narrow staircase with uneven steps.

They went up to the second floor. Rosita took out a key and opened one of the doors to let Frankie through.

"Home at last, Antonio," said Rosita, contentedly. "Make yourself at home, honey."

Frankie found himself in a little living-room fitted with two red plastic armchairs, a table covered with an oilcloth which was full of cigarette burns, and an old television set. On the floor was a carpet of indeterminate colour. The walls were papered with huge carnivorous flowers.

"Rosendo, is that you, son?"

Frankie turned his head to where the voice was coming from. Through a half-open door he could see an old woman with a yellow face, lying on a bed.

"Coming, mummy, I'll be with you in a minute," replied Rosita.

Frankie sat down. So here he was — stranded in the house of a fat homosexual — and just about to smoke his first joint. For the time being he felt no urgency about anything. All he wanted was a bit of comfort — to talk about all the things that he'd missed out on in life, and all the things he was never going to achieve.

"Antonio, love, would you like me to make you a coffee?"

"Sure, thanks."

Rosita disappeared off into the kitchen. Frankie could hear her singing snatches of a bolero.

They sat down to drink their coffee, facing each other in the half light of the sitting-room. Rosita got up to turn on the radio, and came back with a little wooden box in her hand. She sat down again and took out something that looked like a small lump of chocolate. She took a Virginia cigarette, moistened the length of it with saliva, split it open and placed the tobacco in the palm of her hand. Frankie watched her in silence.

Rosita began to singe the little lump with a lighter. Then she mixed it in with the tobacco, passed it to her other hand and took a cigarette paper. She rolled it all together in the paper, stuck it down and said:

"There you go. You're going to like this."

Frankie stared at the joint like it was a .44 pistol pointed at his head.

Rosita stripped off her jacket and sat there with a bare torso. She had two large floppy breasts. She gave Frankie a coquettish wink, and lit the joint.

"Rosita... I've got so many things to tell you, but I haven't talked with anyone for ages... and I don't know where to begin. You see, I..."

"Stop worrying, honey. Just have a little smoke, and you'll find you can talk easier."

"Are you sure?"

"Of course I'm sure," Rosita assured him, as she passed the joint. Frankie took it a bit nervously, looked at it, plucked up courage and took a puff.

"Tastes OK..." he said, feeling more relaxed.

"Go on, honey, smoke it. It's good for the soul."

A strange smile appeared on Frankie's lips. He felt as if he was flying on a magic carpet over the minarets of a sleeping city. He settled himself more comfortably in the plastic armchair and let his mind wander, unfolding like a strange flower.

Rosita's right nipple was like a pink eye watching him. He began to feel thirsty. He noticed that his heart was pounding like a runaway train. A chill fear was invading his body. Maybe he'd end up dying in this chair. He imagined himself dressed in white and sitting on a rainbow looking down at earth. And at that moment his wife began talking to him from the radio.

"Frankie, darling, I know you're there, so listen. You don't know how much it hurts me to be without you, and how much I want to be back with you, but I'm scared to see you after so much time.

"I'd like to stroke your face and kiss you, and make love with you, and wake up by your side just like before.

"I can't stand it any more, Frankie, I need to be with you. I'll never forgive myself for the mistake I made when I left you.

"Can you hear me, darling... ? Can you hear me?"

Frankie noticed that his wife's hand was on his cock. He could feel her body pressing up against his. The banana smell of her perfume enveloped him with infinite tenderness, and she touched his chest through his open shirt.

He let her do it.

He shut his eyes and registered that his wife was very slowly pulling down the zip of his jeans. He could hardly believe it — it had been so long without her. He kissed her plump breasts as they pressed against his face, and noticed that his cock was out of his jeans.

"Darling, you're back... " Frankie murmured.

It was all marvellous. He opened his legs a bit wider so that her lips could reach his sex.

His wife loved him. Never again would he let her go.

Frankie let himself sink back into the armchair, grasped her rough-feeling hair, and let out a hoarse groan when his cock discharged into Rosita's thirsty mouth.

4

F rankie got back to the hotel at midnight: two hours
late for work. When he left Rosita's house, he'd gone
to sleep it off in a cinema in the barrio. He felt tired,
dirty and cheated. This was the last time he'd ever ask help
from anybody. All he had left now was Natalia, and maybe
Senora Hortensia...

When he opened the door he found Manolo in his chair.
He was eating a chorizo sandwich, and had a bottle of
wine on the table.

"For fuck's sake, Frankie, you're overdoing it a bit..."

"I'm sorry, Manolo, I ran into some problems..."

"You mean you ran into a woman!"

"That's my business."

Manolo clicked his tongue, drank some wine from the
bottle and then said in a low voice:

"You've missed all the fun, pal."

"Fun? What's happened? Has the Lizard turned up?"

"No, it's the girl."

Frankie took a chair and sat next to Manolo at the table.
He knew that something had happened to Natalia.

"Come on then, tell me."

"She's cleared off."

"What?"

"That's right. She left you a note on the table. Here it is."

Manolo handed over a small pencil-written note.
Frankie snatched it from his hand and anxiously started to
read:

ANTONIO. THE BABY HAS DIED. I AM LEAVING.
NATALIA.

Frankie stood silent for a minute or two, contemplating
the note. Manolo watched him, intrigued.

"I'm going to have to find her," Frankie murmured to
himself.

"If I were you, I'd forget her, pal. You know how chicks
are. Here today and gone tomorrow... She'll be back as
soon as she needs a meal or a roof over her head."

"Did you see her go?"

Manolo shook his head.

"The kid's sick. She needs someone to be with her; she
can't go wandering the streets alone."

"Well she must have gone somewhere, eh?"

"We'll have to do something... Inform the police,
maybe..."

"For fuck's sake," Manolo interrupted. "You don't even
know her name."

"Doesn't matter. She's not hard to recognize. She's
probably wandering round the Ramblas, or sitting on a
bench in Plaza Real. Who knows..."

Manolo shrugged his shoulders, picked his teeth with
a toothpick from behind his ear, and absent-mindedly
scratched his left armpit.

"So what do you expect me to say, Frankie?"

"She can't have gone far. I'm going out to look for her."

"Now?"

"Yes, now."

"And who's going to look after the hotel?" Manolo asked
in alarm.

"You."

"Don't fuck about, Frankie."

"Look, Manolo, tell you what... If you wait here till I
get back, I'll bring you the latest *Playboy*. All right?"

Manolo hesitated for a moment.

"OK... But I'd rather have *El Lib...*"

"Fine, you'll get both of them."

"You sure you won't forget?"

"Sure."

"I'm worn out, pal. I tell you, I've spent all day in here."

"I won't be long; I'll just take a stroll to see if I can find her."

"Could you get me some cigarettes?"

"Sure, Manolo. See you," said Frankie, and out he rushed, in search of Natalia.

Frankie headed towards the bright lights of the bars on the Ramblas. A gallery of unknown faces flickered up before him like characters in a horror film. As he walked his muscles were tense and his nerves on edge like those of a condemned man. His hands were wedged in his pockets. His shirt was damp round the armpits. He looked anxious and morose. A cigarette hung from his mouth.

He stopped at every intersection to look up and down the street. He stopped off for a beer in a couple of bars, and stood staring out onto the street. He was sure that he'd never see the girl again, but he felt he had to go on trying to find her.

He looked at everyone and everything.

He checked out the rent boys at the Liceo subway station. He watched the girls go by, curly-headed and showing white knickers through thin dresses. He watched plainclothes policemen — all casual jackets, dark glasses and unconvincing moustaches — as they walked up and down, very sure of themselves, and very obvious. He watched henpecked husbands drinking iced lemonade on café terraces next to fat, sleepy wives. He watched obstreperous, red-eyed drunks as they cursed the full moon.

Natalia was nowhere to be seen.

Frankie sat down on a bench, lit a cigarette and tried to think. A painful notion was taking shape in his head.

He tried to think about something else, but it was no good.
Natalia needed money, and there's only one easy way for
a girl to get money. Natalia was probably selling her body.

He leapt to his feet and moved off down the Ramblas.
He was convinced that this was where he'd find her. He
imagined her in a mini-skirt, leaning up in the doorway
of some hotel, calling out after passing men. He was going
crazy. He began to walk faster. He saw the prostitutes as
he reached Plaza Teatro. The square was full of them.

Some were standing out on the pavement, others were
sitting on car bonnets, others were sitting in bars, some
were up some nearby alley, and some were elsewhere,
hard at work.

He'd have to review the troops.

Frankie stopped in front of one of girls. Not much more
than a kid, not much to look at, and visibly
undernourished. She had a bored look, and the name of
a man tattooed on her right arm.

"Mind if I ask you something?" he asked, timidly.

"Sure."

"It's about a girl... She's run away from home, and..."

"You not the Law, are you...?" she interrupted.

"No, I promise you. She's really pretty, you know, but
she's a bit cross-eyed. She's sixteen years old, and her
name's Natalia. I just wondered if you'd seen her around."

The kid gave him a look that said she didn't know.

"How should I know, pal, there's so many of us... I don't
think I've seen anyone cross-eyed, though..."

Frankie tensed his lips.

"OK, thanks, I'll just carry on looking."

"Hey, wait a second."

"What?"

"Do you fancy coming up for a quick screw?"

"Not right now. Some other time, maybe."

"Come on! It'll do you good," she insisted, taking him
by the arm.

"I'm sorry, I've got to go," said Frankie, returning to his search.

At three in the morning he decided to pack it in. In some ways he was happy he hadn't found Natalia. He'd spent a long hour watching the whores going in and out of the hotels. He looked like one of those poor sods who stand there on street corners just watching, not doing anything, or maybe timing how long it takes for the girls to get shot of their customers.

He was just about to cross the street when he happened to turn his head one last time. It was then that he saw her, coming down the steps of a hotel. She was wearing a black dress with a slim gold belt. She was wearing golden high-heeled shoes. She looked a bit paler than before. She had her hair pulled tightly back. She was sporting electric-blue eye-shadow and iodine-red lipstick. Dressed to kill.

Frankie managed to turn his back to her, and stood there on the pavement, staring into the gutter. Pandemonium had suddenly exploded in his brain. He had just seen the woman who had been, who still was, his wife.

All of a sudden Frankie began to run. It was all he could do. The main thing was to get away from the place. A strange sensation drove him forward, as if it wasn't his own volition that was making him run, but his feelings for all the people that he'd ever loved. He shot up the Ramblas like a rocket. He felt neither fear nor fatigue. His mind was a blank. He didn't look at the people he passed. He bumped into a woman who was selling cigarettes, and knocked her over. He heard insults shouted at him as he passed. An anonymous hand tried to stop him, grabbing at his shirt. One of the sleeves tore. He ran on. For a moment he thought he heard a siren. When he reached the corner of Calle Fernando, he found himself suddenly paralysed by an impeccable armlock administered by an officer of the law.

This cop was immediately joined by another, and they

began to search him. Frankie was bathed in sweat. The sleeve of his shirt hung in tatters. He looked like a man who had just snatched somebody's handbag.

"OK, pal," said one of them. "Why were you running like that?"

"I've done nothing... I was just going home."

"Can I see your papers?"

"Yes, here you are."

Frankie handed over his ID card. People were beginning to gather. The cop cast a rapid glance over the card, but he didn't give it back.

"Where do you work?"

"I'm a night porter in a hotel."

"At this time of night you ought to be at work."

"Yes, but I had to come out for a bit."

"Racing up and down the Ramblas like a lunatic?"

"I was looking for a girl."

The cop was obviously not satisfied. He looked at his fellow officer and shook his head.

"You'd better accompany us to the car," he said, finally.

"Why?"

"So's we can find out if you've got a record."

"I haven't, honest..."

"We'll see. Come along."

They put him on the back seat of the police car, one cop on either side. Another cop sat in the front seat. He had Frankie's ID in his hand. He was talking into a radio.

"Charlie 4 to Tango X, over..."

"Tango X, come in Charlie 4... Over."

"Run a check on Antonio Castro Fernandez. Over."

"Charlie 4. Repeat name. Over."

They continued in this vein, like they were in the army.

"Do you mind if I smoke?" Frankie asked.

"Wait."

Five minutes later, Tango X called back.

"Tango X to Charlie 4... Over."

"Charlie 4. Come in Tango X. Over."

"Antonio Castro Fernandez. Record clear."

Frankie breathed a sigh of relief. The cop turned to him and handed him his ID card.

"OK, you can go. Next time you need to take a run, go to the mountains."

"Yes... all right... goodnight."

"Goodnight."

He got out of the police car and walked up the street a bit. Was he going to return to the hotel, or was he better off just lying down in a doorway and never getting up again. He couldn't go far in his present pitiful state. Anyway, Manolo would be waiting for him. In spite of everything, he managed to remember the magazines. He went up to a news kiosk, bought them, and decided that this must have been the worst day of his life. And the future didn't look a lot brighter, either.

Manolo had fallen asleep with his arms on the table and his head resting on his arms. He'd left the radio on, and a cigarette was burning away in the ashtray. At that moment he woke up and looked at Frankie like he was a stranger.

"...She's gone..." he said, in a puzzled voice.

"Who's gone?"

"Um... I don't know... The blonde..."

He'd been dreaming about women again. He had this kind of dream two or three times a week.

"Here you are, here's your magazines, Manolo. You can go to bed now."

Manolo rubbed his eyes, yawned, and finally noticed Frankie.

"What's happened to your shirt?" he asked, intrigued.

"Nothing. I just tore the sleeve."

"You been in a fight?"

Frankie didn't answer. He just wanted to be left alone.

"What about the kid?" Manolo asked.

"No sign of her. Do me a favour, go to bed, will you?"

"OK, pal, as you like..."

Manolo got up stiffly, yawned again, took his magazines and wandered off to his room. He would spend the night surrounded by beautiful paper women.

"See you in the morning, Frankie," he called down the gloomy corridor.

"See you."

Frankie took off his torn shirt and checked the keys on the board. There was nobody to wait up for. He sat in his chair and toyed with some breadcrumbs on the table. He got up, went to the kitchen to empty the ashtray, and came back with a plate of boiled greens from the fridge. They were cold, but it was too much effort to warm them up. They were uneatable. He looked at the phone at his elbow. He stuck his hand in the back pocket of his jeans and took out the card with Hortensia's phone number. It was 4.20 in the morning. He picked up the phone, held it in his hand for a moment, and realized that he was on the verge of tears and about to start talking to himself. He imagined that his wife would be going home by now. In one single rapid movement he took the phone, dialled the number, closed his eyes and waited. Moments later he heard a woman's voice.

"Hello..."

Frankie was suddenly lost for words.

"Hello, who's there?"

There was a short pause. He had to say something, or she'd hang up.

"It's Antonio."

"Oh..."

"I'm sorry if I woke you up."

"No... it's just that... I wasn't expecting... at this time of night..."

"I'm sorry. Really."

"Don't worry. I was awake. As I told you, I can't sleep

at nights," she said, beginning to sound less nervous.

"I had to talk with someone, you see. That's why I took the liberty of phoning."

"I'm happy that you thought of me."

"I've had a very hard day, Senora Hortensia, and..."

"You can call me Hortensia, if you like," she interrupted.

Frankie smiled slightly. He was beginning to feel better. He liked the sound of this woman's voice.

"All right, Hortensia. Honestly, it's done me good to call you, and the fact that you're willing to listen to me, eh."

"Why, did you think I wouldn't?"

"I don't know... It is very late..."

"Seems to me like you're a bit nervous."

"That's an understatement."

"What's happened, Antonio?"

"Well, it's all a bit complicated. I'd rather explain when I see you."

"So you're coming on Sunday, then?" she asked enthusiastically.

"Yes, sure."

"Veal casserole?"

"Whatever suits you best, Hortensia."

"Shall we say three o'clock?"

"That's fine. I'll bring a bottle of wine."

"I don't drink, Antonio, but if you want to..."

"No, it's all right. Water's better for you anyway."

"Are you still drinking a lot?"

"Not by choice. People force me into it."

"You have to be a bit firmer with yourself, Antonio."

"Honestly, it's not my fault."

"Can I tell you something?"

"Sure."

"You know what, I think I'm feeling a bit sleepy."

"Oh, I'm sorry... I didn't..."

"No, please, don't get me wrong. I meant that talking

with you seems to have relaxed me; now I think I might even get an hour or two's sleep."

"I know what you mean. It's the same with me. I haven't been able to eat a thing all day, and now I'm feeling hungry."

"Have you got any food in the hotel?"

"Boiled greens."

"Is that all?"

"I think so. Since you're tired now, make the most of it and get some sleep. I won't keep you any longer."

"But I told you, I'm very happy that you rang."

"All right, that's fine then. Anyway, we'll see each other on Sunday. Sleep well."

"Thank you very much, Antonio. Good night."

"Good night, Hortensia," said Frankie, as he put the phone down and went off to heat up the greens.

5

Dear Fellow Member,
    I won't beat about the bush. I'm writing to you
    because you've got a sympathetic face and I've
taken a liking to you. I'm not usually wrong about
people. Anyway, you live in Barcelona, and that's good
enough for me. I'll tell you why.

What a weird bunch of people they are in this club.
Each one's worse than the next. They all look like
they've never had a decent meal in their lives. And as
for the women, well, most of them wouldn't even rate
a date with the village idiot. For sure, the second letter
you get from them is already talking about marriage.

I'm going to tell you why I decided to join the club.

A month ago I came out of nick. I did five years in
Carabanchel. Armed robbery. Could be worse. One
thing I know, I'm not going back there. I'd rather croak
first. And another thing, if you don't like my story, you
can take the paper and wipe your arse with it! OK?

To continue.

Right now I'm flat broke. I don't have a cent, and I
spend all day in a lousy flat that a friend's lent me. I
want to leave Madrid and get something going in
Barcelona. But as you know, without funds, you can't
do a thing. When I'm out in the street, I tell people that
I'm unemployed, and I ask for a hundred pesetas. If I'm
in luck, it's a beer in some cheap bar.

What a fit-up! What a shitty life!

When I first saw the club's advert, I couldn't believe my eyes. What are things coming to? These days if you want to get a woman, you have to join clubs and write letters to people!

But then I thought about it a bit. Maybe I'd meet someone in the know who would give me the lowdown on the Barcelona rackets. Or I'd team up with an unattached lady teacher and never do another fucking day's work in my life.

What I can't stand is not having anything. It's not that I want to spend twelve hours a day at work, but all I do at the moment is lie in bed smoking Celtas and going out of my skull.

I'm feeling the need to talk to someone. And to go to a Chinese restaurant. And to spend a few days in the Canaries with a nice blonde in tow. I want to buy a decent shirt. To get blind drunk on Cuba Libres in a discotheque. To have a bit of dough. Not to feel like an old stiff.

Seems to me that I'm giving you a hard time. Anyway, if you feel like it, why don't you write to me. And if not, go scratch yourself with a broken bottle!
Juan Cuevas Heredia.

Frankie finished reading the first of the three letters that had arrived that morning. He was waiting his turn at the barber's. There were two other customers in front of him. He didn't know whether to carry on and read the other letters, or forget about the club altogether. He needed a break. He looked at himself in one of the barber's faded old mirrors, and the twisted smile came back to his lips. The ghosts of Natalia and his wife had been temporarily laid, and the next day Senora Hortensia would be waiting for him. He picked up one of the magazines from under the barber's table and leafed through it. Sinatra was performing in Vegas. He looked at the photo for a minute

or two, and then took another look at himself in the mirror.
He put down the magazine, pulled out the second letter
and began reading.

Dear Antonio Castro:
I am three feet four inches tall, I weigh seven stone and
I'm twenty-two years old. I'm blonde, and I've got blue
eyes. My name is Begonia Montana. I thought I ought
to start my letter with the most important things,
because I don't like leading people on. As you can
imagine, I've not had a particularly easy life, but I have
tried to get over my problem, and now I understand
that there are more important things in life than one's
looks. I live with my sister in a little village, and I earn
my living giving English lessons. I have many friends
in the village, and even though they're a bit strange
with me sometimes, I understand them because maybe
in their place I would do the same. I've never been out
with boys, and I've never been in love with anyone.
I've always been a very private sort of person, but
gradually I have come to accept myself as I am, and not
worry about what people think of me.

The thing I like best in life is writing poetry, and at
the moment I'm trying to finish a book. I know that it's
going to be very difficult to get it published, but I'll do
my best.

I also like going to the pictures a lot, particularly
American films, and I want to tell you that the reason
why I wrote is because I think you look very much like
Frank Sinatra.

My reason for joining the club is so I can commun-
icate with people, get to know them, exchange ideas,
and meet new friends.

I don't know whether you're the sort of person who
likes poetry, but anyway I've decided to send you one of
my poems.

I am alone in the night,
Dreaming of sleeping swallows,
Far-off cities and blue bells.
The stars watch over me in peace,
And I converse with them,
I tell them of my life.
I have no pain in my blood,
And no grief in my gaze,
Nor anger in my words.
I don't know if I am happy,
But at this moment
I can sing a song which is my own,
And that's enough.

When you write, I would really like it if you told me what you thought of my poem, and if the subject interests you I think we could find a lot to talk about.

There are other things that I meant to tell you, but I think I would rather that we get to know each other a bit better first. I've been in the club for a year and a half now, and often people have written to me in a less than decent manner, particularly men, but I am sure that the same thing is not going to happen with you.
Awaiting your reply,
Yours affectionately,
Begonia Montana.

"What's up, Frankie? Bad news?" Camacho, the barber, was peering at him through his tinted glasses. He had interrupted his work.

"No... why?"

"You're white as a sheet."

"I've not been sleeping well."

"If you ask me, what you need is a woman."

"Do me a favour, don't say that word."

"Here, have a drink," said Camacho as he walked away

from his customer. He took a bottle of wine from one of the shelves and handed it to Frankie.

Camacho was an alcoholic. He was noted for drinking on the job, but he still had a steady hand when it came to shaving and cutting. He'd never yet cut anybody's throat!

When he finished work, he usually went to a nearby *bodega* and carried on drinking while he played cards or dominos. He was a tall, stooping figure, not far off fifty. He had a face like a camel and wore a pair of enormous bottle-green glasses. His wife had died several months previously and now he lived alone with his tortoise. His breath stank. Frankie hesitated for a moment, and then said:

"OK, give me a drink."

Camacho smiled contentedly. "Finish the bottle. I've got another one out back."

Frankie took a long swig, lit a cigarette at the filter end by mistake, stubbed it out, and then, with a slightly unsteady hand, opened the third envelope.

Brother Antonio:
I have joined this club because of the immense pity and overflowing love which I feel towards all creatures on earth. I too lived in the wilderness of loneliness until, by the grace of the Lord, I came to know God's infinite goodness. It is for this reason that I want to guide you all up the golden path of truth and boundless love which is so close at hand.

For years now I have been communing with the Lord Jesus and with the Virgin Mary. They are very upset about mankind, about man's folly, his egotism and his cruelty.

I can tell you that I myself, with a handkerchief that I keep as a relic, have dried the tears which the Virgin Mary spilled on my shoulder. And I have seen Jesus

Christ bleeding from his wounds, looking at us sadly, but without losing his faith in the final destiny of us all.

I also have many little angels, who fly around my room, singing their golden hymns. But what worries me most, Brother Antonio, is that the Virgin Mary has told me that the Wicked One has incarnated himself in a man whose name she does not know, but who is a member of this club.

I am sure that we shall all attain eternal salvation if we can find the Wicked One and destroy him.

I am sure that you, like the other members of our club, will help me in finding him. I entreat you to let me know if you see any sign of the Wicked One.

Let us help the Virgin Mary to stop crying!

Finally, I want to tell you, Brother Antonio, that as from now you will be present in my prayers, and I shall endeavour to help you to a happier life. May the Lord bless you!

Brother Blanco Sol.

Camacho had just finished trimming his last customer, and he gestured to Frankie to get into the chair.

"Your turn."

"They're persecuting me, Camacho..."

"What do you mean?"

"I can't stand it any more. It's driving me crazy."

Camacho looked at him in silence, adjusted his glasses with his ring-finger, consulted his watch, turned his head to the street, and said:

"Hang on a minute, it's time for me to shut up shop."

The barber turned round the little "closed" sign that hung in his door, locked up, and came back to Frankie.

"Right, do you want me to cut your hair or not?"

"I suppose so."

"Well, what are you waiting for?"

Frankie got up, put the letter in his pocket, and settled

into the barber's chair.

"Look, Frankie, if you ask me, you need someone to talk to. If you want, I'm willing to listen. OK?"

Frankie nodded.

"I've just received three letters, Camacho. One from an armed robber who's fresh out of prison, another from a dwarf who writes poetry, and another from some kind of nutter who claims to have conversations with Jesus. I tell you, it's cracking me up."

Camacho's scissors paused in mid-air for a moment, and then continued with their work.

"Are you serious?"

"I've joined a lonely hearts club."

"What was I saying, Frankie? You need a girlfriend."

"A woman from the club has invited me for Sunday lunch tomorrow."

Camacho's face showed the traces of a sceptical smile.

"Things like that tend to turn out badly..."

"What do you think I should do, then?"

"I don't know. Learn to sit and wait, I suppose..."

"You waiting for anything out of life?"

"Every week for the last thirty years that I've been stuck in this damn barber shop, I've bought a lottery ticket. That's the only thing I want out of life — to win the jackpot."

"Have you ever thought of finding another woman?"

"I've had enough of women, Frankie. These days I prefer to stick to wine and tortoises."

The conversation lapsed until Camacho had finished his work. Frankie took a last swig of wine with the barber, paid him, and went back to the hotel.

As he came through the front door, he found the Lizard wandering round on his own.

He was an ancient little man with a mould-coloured face and evil little snake's eyes. His bald head was spotted with purple blotches. From his nostrils emerged a variety of black and white hairs. His mouth was thin and dry. At the corners of his mouth you could see the occasional drop of spittle. He had a bulbous potato nose, shot through with little red veins.

He wore a short-sleeved black shirt that displayed his skinny arms. An enormous belt strangled his trousers around an equally skinny waist.

His flies were open.

"I was waiting for you, Antonio," he said, by way of greeting.

His voice seemed to come from the depths of some ancient Egyptian tomb.

"How are you, Senor Flores?"

The Lizard stretched his lips into what was presumably a smile.

"How do I look?"

"You're looking very well, Senor Flores."

"You're wrong."

"I'm sorry to hear it, Senor Flores."

"Come on, let's sit down for a moment. I need to talk to you," said the Lizard, as he took Frankie's arm in his bony claw.

Frankie was assailed by an instant sense of foreboding. He sat down at the table in the dingy reception area, and the Lizard settled into an armchair.

"Are you happy in your work, Antonio?" the Lizard asked, casually.

"Of course, Senor Flores."

"I'm glad to hear it, because these are difficult times and jobs like this are not easy to find."

"Yes, Senor Flores."

"Right, then. What I wanted to say is... I'm getting on a bit, and..."

"You're looking very fit, though, Senor Flores," said Frankie, lying.

"Don't smooth-talk me! And what's more, you can stop all that 'Senor Flores' nonsense. You think I don't know that everyone in the hotel calls me the Lizard?"

Frankie kept silent.

"As I was saying," the Lizard continued. "For a man of my age there are a lot of things that are not easy... Women, for instance. You get my meaning?"

Frankie shuddered. He couldn't see quite what the Lizard was getting at.

"What's more, I don't have a lot of friends. You see, I'm looking for someone to take me somewhere where there are girls. To a dance maybe, or a nightclub. I've never fancied going out on my own, you know what I mean?"

"Where do I come into it?" asked Frankie in a weak voice.

"You could come with me."

This confirmed Frankie's fears. The Lizard was losing his marbles.

"I have to work, though, senor."

"That's no problem. Manolo can do the night shift."

"And tomorrow I've got a very important appointment."

"Look, Antonio, I'll make it easy. If you don't come with me tonight, then tomorrow you pack your bags and go."

Frankie was cornered. He had no choice.

"As you wish," he said, after a brief pause.

The Lizard seemed satisfied. He took a handkerchief out of his trouser pocket, blew his nose, looked at Frankie again and attempted a smile.

"Will you take me to a disco?" he asked, slily.

"Wouldn't it be better if we went to the pictures?"

"Come off it, Antonio, how are we going to meet girls at the pictures?"

The Lizard glanced briefly at his gold watch, got up from his chair and said in an authoritative voice:

"I'll be expecting you at the Café de L'Opéra, at eleven o'clock."

"I'll be there," Frankie replied, collapsing over the table.

Frankie left the hotel at five to eleven. He didn't have the first idea where he could take the Lizard, or what he might do with him. It had been years since he'd last been in a nightclub, let alone with an old man of eighty-three.

The Lizard was drinking mint with soda. It seemed that this was not his first. He had a lighted cigar in his mouth and was smiling to himself.

"You're very punctual, Antonio!"

"I didn't want to keep you waiting," said Frankie, as he sat down next to him.

"Would you like a drink, or shall we go straight to the disco?"

"The trouble is... you know what the problem is, Senor Flores? I don't know any discos. I thought that maybe we could go to a bingo hall and..."

"Don't worry, Antonio. I'll arrange it, no problem."

The Lizard turned his head and clicked his fingers to summon the waiter.

"Sir?" asked the waiter.

"Come here, I want to ask you something."

"Fire away, sir."

"Do you know any decent discotheques around these parts?"

The waiter was obviously thrown by this, and tried to catch Frankie's eye.

"I don't know, sir... It depends..."

"There must be plenty in this part of town," the Lizard insisted.

"Well, in fact I usually go to one that's over by Plaza Real, but I don't know whether you..."

"Fine. Don't worry. We'll find it. What do you think, Antonio?"

Frankie attempted a smile, and shrugged agreement.

The club was in a large white basement. It had a long bar with a dozen stools ranged along it. Three or four arches gave onto the dance floor. To the right of the dance floor stood a few tables, and to the left a small stage which was used on nights when there was live music. Spotlights — neon-blue, space-pink, ice-purple and fire-yellow — were criss-crossing the dance-floor like flashing missiles. The loudspeakers were blaring out wild rock and roll. Everybody was dancing or moving. Facing each other. Not touching each other. Not looking at each other. Not laughing either. Some people were shaking their heads as if they were trying to shake them off their shoulders and couldn't get rid of them. Others were jumping all over the place and letting out strange sounds to attract attention to themselves, and nobody even looked. Others moved slowly and mechanically, like Frankenstein, with eyes bulging and their arms rigid, looking like they were about to commit murder. Others shuffled around listlessly with their backs to everyone, as if they were trying to kiss the wall.

Everyone seemed to be dancing alone.

Frankie contrived to settle the Lizard at one of the less conspicuous tables.

"What do you think of it, Senor Flores?" he asked, apprehensively.

The Lizard was looking like some ancient mummy who had just woken up in a world that was unreal and unfamiliar.

"Get me a mint with soda, Antonio," he said with difficulty.

"Don't you think you've had enough to drink, Senor Flores?"

"Who cares?"

Frankie turned to call a waiter, but his eye was suddenly caught by a young girl who was leaning, glass in hand, against one of the arches. He couldn't see her face, but that wasn't important. The thing was, her hair...

An enormous mass of golden hair. A waterfall of locks, some green, some red, some yellow. They moved on the girl's shoulders like a magic spider, with a life of its own, and a sweet and mysterious smell.

The Lizard had seen her too. He grasped Frankie's arm.

"Look, Antonio, look..."

Frankie couldn't say a word. A beam of blue light split the Lizard's face at regular intervals. The smell of the girl's hair was becoming more intense.

"I don't believe it," was all that Frankie could murmur.

At that moment, the girl began dancing, and began to shake her wonderful head of hair. Carefree, she looked unreal. As if her hair was the beginning of everything.

"I knew that I'd find her," the Lizard said to himself, and slowly he got up from his chair.

"Can I get you something, Senor Flores?" Frankie asked.

The Lizard wasn't listening. His eyes were devouring the girl and her hair.

"I think it'd be better if we left," Frankie insisted, suddenly worried.

The Lizard was now on his feet. For a moment he stood there, motionless, leaning on the table; then he made a move towards the dance floor.

"Senor Flores!" Frankie shouted.

Like some heart-broken ghost, the Lizard went over to the girl. He shut his eyes, plunged his hands into the richness of her hair, flattened his face in the entrails of that golden tarantula, opened his mouth to drown himself in the smell of life, and then dropped to the floor, stone dead.

6

Frankie took the two o'clock train to Mataró, for Sunday lunch with Senora Hortensia. He sat next to the window and lit a cigarette. This was his first moment of relaxation since the previous night. He had great purple bags under his eyes. He couldn't take his mind off the Lizard. In some sense he felt guilty. However, he decided that everything in the hotel would probably carry on as normal. It would be inherited by the Lizard's only sister, a sixty-two-year-old spinster.

The train set off, and as it neared his destination, his impending encounter with Senora Hortensia began to unnerve him.

He'd gone for the brown shirt and a pair of blue trousers that he'd retrieved from the cleaners. He'd cut his cheek while shaving, and his face now sported a small sticking plaster. Manolo had loaned him his deodorant and a bottle of aftershave.

Tiredness was creeping up on him, and he half-closed his eyes. He was worried that he'd fall asleep on the train and wake up miles down the line. It finally got the better of him, and he fell asleep, surrendering himself to a dream that was short but intense.

He found himself alone in the abandoned hotel. All of a sudden, he saw Juan Cuevas Heredia coming in through the window with a gun in his hand.

"Get a move on, Frankie," he said, "we're going to hold up the bar."

"We mustn't," Frankie replied. "Brother Blanco Sol will be angry."

"Too bad, let's go."

Next, he saw a small bar where the only light was a solitary candle. Dark shapeless forms huddled round the tables. He heard feeble sounds of lamenting and groaning.

"This is a hold-up!" yelled Juan Cuevas Heredia.

But everybody ignored him.

Frankie took a red lamp and went over to the bar. His wife was behind the counter, naked, drying a glass with a pair of black knickers.

"What d'you want to drink, Frankie?" she asked him, with a smile.

Juan Cuevas Heredia left his gun on a bar stool and went off to the toilet, arm in arm with a blonde dwarf.

Frankie asked his wife for a beer, and went off to search for Natalia among the people sitting at the tables.

"Here I am, Antonio," said Natalia. "I'm married now, to Brother Blanco Sol."

"And I've written them a poem as a wedding present," added Begonia Montana.

"Drink up, Frankie," his wife urged him.

Juan Cuevas Heredia came out of the toilet, picked up the gun and shot himself in the stomach.

"That was a pretty stupid thing to do," Frankie commented, turning to Natalia.

"I have made the Virgin Mary cry," wailed Brother Blanco Sol.

Rosita came into the bar and started crying on Frankie's shoulder.

"I can't sing, Antonio. I'm not the woman I used to be."

At that moment, Juan Cuevas Heredia got up, grabbed a bottle, and told them all:

"I'm bored with being dead."

Camacho, the barber, was playing cards with his tortoise in a corner of the bar. He had a strange smile on his lips.

Frankie was lavishing kisses on Natalia's eyes.

"I love you, kid," he whispered in her ear.

The Lizard's head suddenly appeared from under one of the bar tables and he started shouting:

"I've done it! At last, I've done it!"

A tuft of golden-blonde hair was hanging from his mouth.

Begonia Montana climbed up onto a chair with an enormous envelope in her hands. She called over to Frankie.

"Here's my latest letter, Antonio. I shall never stop writing to you."

And, little by little, all of them left, silently, until the light of the candle went out and once again all that could be heard was a subdued sound of sobbing.

"We're going. We're going... " they said, as each of them passed close to Frankie without touching him.

"Don't leave me on my own, please!" shouted Frankie in the darkness of the bar.

"Anything wrong?"

Frankie opened his eyes to find the ticket inspector standing in front of him.

"No... No... I think I must have been dreaming," he replied, smiling feebly.

"Can I see your ticket, please?"

"Yes, sure. Have we reached Mataró yet?" he asked, nervously.

"Next stop, sir."

Frankie gave a sigh of relief.

"Thanks," he said as the inspector gave back his ticket.

The train pulled into Mataró station. Frankie got off and checked the time on the station clock. He had time for a quick beer at the station. The old fear was creeping up on him again. Now he wasn't dealing with letters or phone calls. Senora Hortensia was actually waiting for him in her house. She'd cooked a meal for him. The food would be ready by now. He wasn't hungry. He was going to find it impossible to eat so much as a mouthful. His stomach had clammed up like a bank-safe. He needed a drink.

By three-twenty, Frankie had already drunk two beers and three gins with ice, and he was still in the station bar. He was twenty minutes late, and he had to make a decision. He could either take the train back to Barcelona, or he'd have to leave the bar immediately.

A few minutes later, Frankie's trembling hand was pressing the doorbell of the small one-storey house where Senora Hortensia lived.

At once he heard the sound of a woman's footsteps coming to the door.

Frankie gritted his teeth and waited.

"Antonio! At last! How are you?"

There stood Senora Hortensia Garcia. She offered him her hand.

"Pleased to meet you, Senora Hortensia," Frankie replied as he shook her hand.

"Come in," she said, smiling.

They looked at each other for a moment or two. She saw a nervous man in a brown short-sleeved shirt and blue trousers, with a wry smile on his lips and good-natured eyes. He seemed kind and harmless enough.

Frankie saw a woman who looked like she wrote cookery books. She had a soft face like a saint on a medallion, and gentle cow's eyes. She'd been to have her hair done. Her breasts were a little on the large side and were imprisoned in a white bra which showed through her pink silk blouse. Her legs were a bit thin and short in relation to the rest of her body. He felt like they'd been married for twenty years.

"I'm so sorry I'm late," Frankie excused himself. "There's always problems with those trains."

"Don't worry, Antonio. Would you like to come in?"

"Of course, thank you."

Frankie found himself in a large, cosy room. There was a substantial wooden table covered with a white, hand-embroidered table cloth. There was a velveteen three-piece suite in front of the colour TV, and the television was on, with the sound turned down. There was a still-life picture hanging on one of the walls. There was a cat fast asleep on a beige cushion. There was a glass cabinet filled with decorated plates and glasses. There was a porcelain vase on a little table. There were shining plates, green bottles of mineral water, sparkling cutlery and neatly folded serviettes. Everything smelt of furniture polish and veal casserole. It was marvellous.

At that moment the voice of Frank Sinatra soared from the record player. He was singing *Let me try it again.*

"I bought it for you, Antonio," said Senora Hortensia, shyly.

"For me?"

"I thought you might like it..."

"I don't know how to thank you, Hortensia... I've never felt so good in all my life."

She inclined her head and gave a satisfied smile. She appeared to know the way to a man's heart.

"Sit down, Antonio. The food's ready."

"Wonderful..."

Senora Hortensia headed off to the kitchen and returned with a bowl of salad, which she placed in the centre of the table. It was a simple salad, with not too many things in it. The tomatoes were red and fresh. The lettuce was fresh too, and speckled with drops of water. The onion had been cut thin, and the olives were just as they should be.

It was a salad which had been made with loving care — which had been made for a special someone.

They began to eat. Senora Hortensia handled her knife and fork as if she was trying not to damage the food. She chewed with her mouth shut. She drank little sips of water, and dried the corners of her mouth with a serviette. Every now and then she would offer up a discreet smile. She didn't say a lot. Frankie was beginning to like her.

He thought that he ought to be talking more. She was waiting.

"I'm very happy that I've come, Hortensia," he said, at last.

"And I am very pleased that you're here."

"You've got a very nice house, you know."

Senora Hortensia decided to take the offensive.

"What do you think of me, Antonio?"

"Well, I..."

"I mean, am I the way you imagined me, or do I seem... different?"

Frankie wavered, took a large sip of water and tried to find an answer.

"I didn't expect that you would be so enjoyable to be with."

She smiled again slightly and lowered her gaze.

"I have something to confess to you, Antonio."

"Fire away."

"You're not the first, you know."

Frankie was momentarily alarmed.

"The first... ? The first what?"

"The first person to come to my house. Other members of the club have been here before you — the last one was only last month."

"I see."

"But I never started a relationship with any of them. They weren't good people. They'd only joined the club in order to meet women and take advantage of them. Both of them wanted the same thing, on the first day."

"Hortensia, I assure you that I..."

"You don't have to tell me, Antonio. You're different."

"I've not had a lot of luck with people from the club either. Except you, of course."

"Sometimes I think that people aren't made to help each other, but just to harm each other, even if they don't always mean to," Senora Hortensia commented, in a tone of sadness.

"That's what I think too."

"Why don't you tell me a bit about yourself, Antonio?"

"I wouldn't know where to start."

"Oh, I am sorry!" she interrupted. "I see you've finished your salad. I'll bring in the casserole."

Frankie smiled contentedly.

"Thank you, Hortensia."

"I'll be back in a second."

Frankie was left alone at the table. He wondered whether he really did like Hortensia. Whether he could make love with her. Whether he wanted her to be his girlfriend.

Maybe it was the tranquillity of her house, the plant hanging in an earthenware pot in a corner of the sitting-room, the Saturday nights that he'd be able to spend with her, sitting and watching a film on her colour TV...

He wasn't too sure of anything, really.

Senora Hortensia returned with the veal casserole. It looked even better than the salad. By now Frankie had completely regained his appetite.

"Here it is, Antonio. I hope you like it."

"I'm sure I will. It's been a long time since a woman last cooked for me."

"You're very lonely, aren't you."

"Like just about everyone else in the world."

She gave a touch to her hair-do.

"Have you never thought of getting married again?"

"Have you, Hortensia?"

"Oh yes, many times," she replied, straightforwardly.

They ate in silence for a minute or two. It seemed to Frankie that the buttons of her blouse were a bit more open than before.

"Look, Antonio," said Senora Hortensia. "I think it

would be best if we put our cards on the table. I know this is our first time together, but I need to talk to you about myself, and particularly about my son. And you probably have a lot of things to tell me too. Why don't we do that?"

Frankie's fork, skewered into a piece of meat, stopped an inch or two from his mouth, and then slowly settled back onto his plate. "You're right, Hortensia," he agreed. "But you know, it's very difficult for me..."

"Try."

Frankie thought of the late and unlamented Lizard. Of his wife coming down the steps of the hotel. Of the little note that Natalia had left him. Of the latest three letters he'd had from the club. And the dream that he'd had on the train...

"I'm sorry, but I can't."

"It'll do you good, Antonio."

Frankie looked her in the eye, and shrugged helplessly. She smiled understandingly.

"Don't worry, you can tell me when you're in the mood to."

"All right, I will."

"I'm very worried about my son, you know..."

Senora Hortensia's words were interrupted by the sound of a key in the front door.

"Oh, God, no... " she murmured.

A violent slam of the door made her shudder.

"Antonio, please..."

"What's going on?" Frankie asked in alarm.

It was as if some murderous hedgehog had erupted into the calm and tranquillity of the living-room. Like a blast from a flamethrower.

The new arrival was a wild adolescent, with a head that was all shaved apart from a red crest of hard spikey hair that stuck up and split his cranium in two. He was encased in a bomber jacket and tight-fitting black leather trousers. He had the look of a psychopath. In fact he gave the impression of being stuffed full of amphetamines. He wore a big steel chain around his waist.

"Rafael, son..." said Senora Hortensia, in a feeble voice.

"Who's this fucking son-of-a-bitch pansy?" hissed the hedgehog.

Senora Hortensia covered her face with her hands and began to cry. The hedgehog began taking his chain off.

"Who is this fucking nancy-boy?" he yelled.

Frankie felt as if he was about to wet himself.

"I asked you a question, bitch!" the hedgehog shouted, as he smashed a lamp with a blow from his chain.

Senora Hortensia stifled a cry.

"He's a friend of mine... I invited him to lunch... We were just talking..." she managed to answer.

"I think it would be best if I went, Hortensia," said Frankie, as he tried to get up from his chair.

"Don't move, creep," the hedgehog ordered.

He had the chain wrapped round his left hand, inches away from Frankie's face.

"Rafael, please, leave us alone," she implored.

"I need some cash. Right now," the hedgehog demanded.

"I've no money today, son, I promise you. Tomorrow I'll give you whatever you need."

The hedgehog turned to Frankie. In his right hand he held a cut-throat razor.

"Please! Rafael!" screamed Senora Hortensia, on the verge of hysteria.

"See here, dick-head, either you hand over the money, or I cut your balls off!"

"All I've got is five hundred pesetas and my return ticket," said Frankie, who by now was thoroughly scared. The hedgehog searched him, took the five hundred-peseta notes and held the razor to his neck. "Now scram, shithead!"

Frankie got up cautiously from the chair and began

moving towards the door.

"Goodbye, Senora Hortensia," he said, feeling rather stupid.

The hedgehog followed him, still holding the razor to his neck.

"If I see you round here again, I'll cut you." So saying, he opened the street-door, aimed a devastating kick at Frankie's arse, and propelled him out into the street.

7

6 and 4, sixty-four... 3 and 8, thirty-eight... 5, number five... 1 and 9, nineteen... 2 and 2, twenty-two... 5 and 0, fifty... 7 and 1, seventy-one..."

A dark-skinned girl with long, jet-black hair was calling the numbers. She had a red dress, the face of an actress in a super-8 porno movie and the legs of an Istanbul whore.

"1 and 4, fourteen... 3, number three... 7 and 5, seventy-five..."

In recent days, Frankie had taken to seeking refuge in bingo halls. He'd sit there, pen in hand, staring at his card and waiting for his luck to change. He'd drink a beer or two, trying to forget, and letting the time pass. Shortly before ten at night he would return to the hotel to start work.

He'd made no further contact with anybody from the club.

"Line!" shouted somebody from one of the nearby tables.

"Somebody called a line?" said the black-haired beauty.

Frankie took another look at her, and chewed on his bottom lip. By now the urgency of getting himself a woman was becoming unbearable. The bingo girl was driving him crazy. He was at a loss what to do.

Again he tried to concentrate on his card. Only a couple of his numbers had come up. And the girl was beginning to obsess him.

Frankie was starting to get a hard-on. His cock was

taking over. The bingo girl was calling the numbers as if they were the numbers of the hotel room where she would be waiting for him.

A weird-looking woman came over to his table. She was dressed in an old mac and plastic sandals. Her hair was grey and dirty, she had a wart on one cheek, and she wore bizarre butterfly glasses. She looked like a tramp. She was leading an idiot child by the hand.

"Excuse me, sir," she said.

"What?"

"How you doing?"

"Badly."

"Not having any luck?"

"No."

"If you like, I'll leave him with you. For a hundred pesetas."

Frankie looked puzzled.

"Leave who for a hundred pesetas?"

The woman pointed to the idiot. The idiot smiled.

"What do I want him for?"

"He brings people luck," she said, murmuring close to Frankie's ear. "If he sits next to you, you're bound to win the jackpot."

"What, d'you mean? You're renting him out?"

"Yes. A hundred pesetas for half an hour."

"Come off it..."

"It's only a hundred pesetas," she said, insistently.

Frankie shrugged his shoulders and smiled. He didn't have much to lose. He put his hand in his pocket and gave the woman the money.

"Thank you, sir. You'll see, he'll help you win — especially if you treat him to an orangeade. That's his favourite drink."

Frankie took a look at the idiot, who sat there smiling.

He had a huge inflated head, yellow eyes like scrambled egg and big purple lips. His body was sickly and disjointed.

He was endlessly eating sunflower seeds. He seemed harmless enough.

"Sit down," said Frankie.

The idiot sat down.

Frankie went and bought a new card, and then called the waiter over. He ordered an orangeade for the idiot and let him be.

A few minutes later, the bingo girl started calling the next batch of numbers. "2 and 4, twenty-four... 1, number one... 3 and 7, thirty-seven... 6, number six..."

By the time someone had called "Line", not even one of Frankie's numbers had come up. At that moment, the waiter arrived with the orangeade, and the idiot began gulping it down.

Seven of Frankie's numbers came up in a row.

"8 and 2, eighty-two... 5 and 9, fifty-nine... 2 and 3, twenty-three..."

Frankie broke into a cold sweat. He couldn't believe it. All he needed now was a forty-five. The girl was still calling numbers. The people sat in silence. The idiot had not yet finished his pop.

"Drink, baby, drink!" Frankie urged.

The idiot looked at him with his customary smile, took the glass and drank. Just then the bingo girl called:

"4 and 5, forty-five."

And Frankie had won seventy-two thousand five hundred pesetas.

When they handed over the money, he went to the bar and ordered up a double whiskey. His legs were shaking. He couldn't believe it.

In fact he didn't need the drink. He was completely drunk on the money. Never in his life had he had so much cash in his pocket. He fondled it. He thought of what he was going to do with it. He felt like singing out loud.

Frankie propped himself with his back to the bar, rested his elbows on the counter, tilted his head to one side, and with a glass of whiskey in one hand surveyed the hall.

He decided he wouldn't be going in to work that night.

"I'm beat," said a voice at his side.

The dark girl with the jet-black hair was standing next to him. She was half talking to herself, but in a voice sufficiently loud for Frankie to hear. She extracted a cigarette from her handbag and took slightly too long finding her lighter. The familiar spiel.

Frankie gave her a light.

"Thanks," she said, trying to appear distant.

"Do you fancy a drink?" Frankie asked.

She gave a slight smile.

"I don't know... Yes, something, I suppose."

"I've just won the jackpot, you know."

"Yes, I saw."

Another girl started calling the numbers.

"Are you finished for the day?"

The girl made a bored gesture.

"I've finished for tonight, but tomorrow it'll be back to the same old grind. It's terrible, you spend all day with your head full of numbers."

"I can imagine..."

"What about you? What do you do?"

"I'm a singer," Frankie answered without batting an eyelid. He finished his whiskey.

"That must be interesting. What's your name?"

"Antonio. What about you?"

"Isabel."

Frankie wondered whether he should ask her out for a meal. He had a notion that women found him particularly attractive. The money was making him bold, and he made up his mind he was going to blow it.

"Tell me something, Isabel."

"What?"

"You doing anything tonight?"

She tried to look surprised.

"Tonight...? No..."

"D'you fancy going out for a meal?" Frankie said, as he ordered another whiskey.

Isabel slowly moved her tongue across her captivating lips. With an infinitely feminine gesture she moved aside a wisp of black hair that was hanging over her right eye. She looked down, blew out the smoke of her cigarette, and said, finally:

"I fancy a bottle of champagne."

"Champagne?"

"I know a nice quiet spot. Real cosy."

"OK," Frankie agreed. "I'll finish my drink, and we'll go."

Isabel took him to a place in the old part of the city. It wasn't bad. It was quiet, not too big, with an elegant bar, red lights, beige flock wallpaper and soft background music.

There were two blondes there, one behind the bar — pretty, but getting on a bit — who was talking with a customer, and another, far younger, who was seated on a bar stool and showing a lot of leg to little effect.

The two of them greeted Isabel. They obviously knew her. Almost as if she worked there.

It reminded Frankie of the bar where he had first met his wife. But this didn't particularly worry him. He ordered a bottle of champagne. Isabel took him by the arm.

"Do you want to drink it here? Or shall we go to a private room?"

"Have they got one?" asked Frankie.

This was a pleasant surprise.

"Sure," said Isabel.

"Let's go, then."

At the end of the bar two or three steps led up to another, smaller, room with more subdued lighting They went up and sat next to each other. It was very comfortable. The seats appeared to be made of leather. The bar-stool blonde appeared with a bottle of champagne in an ice bucket.

Frankie couldn't get the grin off his face. He was loving it. He was sure they were going to fleece him of his last cent, but he didn't care. Isabel was marvellous. He'd never been with such a woman. He imagined what it would be like to wake up in bed with her. Opening his eyes and finding her there, warm, naked, beautiful, and ready for a quick one.

They drank their first glass in silence. Isabel had crossed her legs. She was one hell of a girl. Frankie started to get physical.

"You live on your own, don't you?" she asked.

"Yes. How do you know?"

"It's obvious."

Frankie kissed her on the lips. She responded, not over-interested, but just sufficiently not to make him feel bad.

"Would you like to spend the night with me?" Isabel asked.

"What's it going to cost me?"

"Twenty thousand... all night..."

"That's a bit pricey..."

"You'll have a good time."

"I don't know why you bother working in the bingo hall."

"I don't like the idea of doing this every night, see. Just once or twice a month. If I did it more often, it would get unbearable."

"Do you fancy me?"

Isabel ruffled his hair like he was a kid.

"Tell me the truth. Do you fancy me?"

She drank a sip of her champagne, lit a cigarette and gave him an amused look.

"A bit," she replied.

Frankie undid her dress, took one of her breasts and began to suck it. It was glorious. Isabel had one hand on the back of his neck, and she let him do it. He moved to the other breast. He couldn't decide which one he liked best.

"Gently, Antonio," she said.

Frankie was beside himself. He was about to come. Isabel guessed this, undid his flies and slowly began to masturbate him.

"Shall I go on?" she asked.

"Please, please, do it... Go on!"

When it was all over, Isabel went to wash her hands in the toilet and Frankie drank another glass of champagne. He'd be going to bed with her. He'd give her all the money she needed. He'd win a bingo jackpot every day. Isabel came back from the toilet and sat down next to him again, kissing him on the cheek.

"How you feeling?" she asked.

"Better than ever."

"Shall we get another bottle of champagne?"

"As many as you want."

Isabel got up and went to the bar to order the champagne. Frankie stretched out on the comfortable seat of their private room, lay back and folded his hands behind his head. He kicked off his shoes. He whistled. For the first time in his life, he was king.

"Look at him! Enjoying himself!" Isabel commented, on her return.

"Come over here, kid," said Frankie, and he sat up a bit. "Sit on my lap."

She did as he said, went over, and settled herself on his knee.

"Are we going to spend the night together, darling?"

Frankie smiled. He liked her calling him darling. He presumed that it would add to his bill.

"What do you think?"

"I think yes."

"Me too."

They were into their second bottle of champagne.

Frankie was telling her all sorts of things. She knew how to listen, too.

Frankie paid the blonde waitress the fifteen thousand for the champagne, and gave five thousand to Isabel for their performance in the private cubicle. They went out into the street and hailed a cab.

The hotel was a seven-storey building, modern and bright, with an enormous neon sign outside. It had a bored porter standing at the front door. Dressed like a general reviewing the troops of the Austro-Hungarian Empire, he strolled up and down on the pavement. There wasn't a lot of sense in his being there, since the hotel doors opened automatically as you approached.

There was air conditioning in the reception and a small bar in another room set off to the right of the entrance. The décor was pink picked out with little black patterns, and the lifts had shiny steel doors.

The manager who greeted them was agreeable, jovial, fair-haired, elegant and obviously efficient. He could have been bred for the job. He knew at a glance that Frankie had won at bingo or something of the sort, but he didn't let on.

"I'd like a double, please," said Frankie.

"Certainly, sir."

The manager turned and took down a key.

"There you are, sir."

Frankie took out the wad of banknotes.

"Thirteen thousand and seven hundred pesetas, sir."

"Fine."

He paid the money.

"Thank you, sir. Good night."

"Good night."

Another hotel flunkey, not so flamboyantly dressed, accompanied them to the lift. It was hardly necessary — it was only a few yards. He opened the door for them. Frankie gave him a five-hundred-peseta tip.

They went up to the fifth floor, their arms round each other as they walked down the corridor. Isabel had her head on his shoulder. Just like in the movies.

It was a five-star hotel room, with a portable television, a low bed covered with a beige bedspread, two comfortable armchairs, a gleaming white fridge, a french window which gave out onto a rectangular balcony, and a bathroom decorated with pink tiles...

For a moment Frankie left Isabel and went to look in the fridge. It was full of splits of champagne, cans of beer, fruit juices, and bottles of mineral water.

Isabel opened the French window and stepped out onto the balcony. Frankie followed her.

The city was spread out below them.

"Shall we have a drink, Antonio?"

"I'm drunk already, but what the hell..."

"What would you like?"

"Anything you fancy."

Frankie lit a cigarette and stood there, alone and unmoving, looking out over Barcelona's electric night.

He listened to the sound of the cars below; his eyes shone with the light reflected from the hotel's vertical neon sign; he wrapped himself in the opaque fog that seemed to settle over the traffic lights and the cement. He thought he saw a shooting star disappearing behind the buildings in the distance, and fell, forever, in love with this moment of his life.

Isabel came up on him from behind and pressed her breasts against his back.

"Are you going to stand there all night?"

Frankie turned round and looked into her eyes. They were like two diamonds in a sea of silver.

"Would you prefer me to pay you now?" he asked.

"I think I'm not going to charge you," she said.

She took him gently by the hand and led him into the room. She turned the main lights out and switched on a small blue bedside lamp. Frankie sat on the bed. Isabel began to get undressed.

It was then that Frankie noticed that she was not undressing in the way a prostitute would undress. She was undressing like a woman about to go to bed with her husband.

"That's the last time they ever fuck about with me," Frankie promised himself as he kicked his shoes off. "They won't fuck about with me ever again."

And he had the wildest night of love-making ever.

8

F rankie sat on the edge of the fountain in Plaza Real
and lit a cigarette. It was seven in the morning. He'd
left Isabel ten minutes previously. He had her phone
number in his shirt pocket. He felt relaxed. He wasn't
tired. All was well with the world.

He gazed absent-mindedly at the switched-off street
lights and the tall palm trees in the deserted square. All
of a sudden his attention was caught by the sight of a thin,
jaundiced-looking girl, her face half covered by an
enormous pair of dark glasses. She was sitting near him,
dabbling her feet in the water of the fountain.

She was wearing a tattered flowery shirt through which
a small breast was visible. She had a pair of too-large grimy
white jeans. She looked as if her hair had been cut by a
lunatic, and she was talking to herself.

All of a sudden she took off her dark glasses and looked
at him. It was Natalia. His problems were about to start
again.

"Antonio..." she murmured.

Frankie was stuck for words.

Natalia came over to him. She moved like a scarecrow,
all skin and bone.

"What's happened to you, Natalia?"

"I can't go on, Antonio. You're going to have to help
me," she said, and she fell into his arms.

Frankie held her without saying a word, focused his
eyes on the middle distance, bit his lip and threw his

cigarette butt into the fountain.

He didn't know what to do.

Natalia began crying, and snuggled up even smaller in his arms.

"Antonio, I need money. I'm on smack. I've got a habit. It's horrible..."

Money — Smack — Habit...

He wondered what she was talking about, and concluded that Natalia was injecting heroin and needed money to get her fix. He took a close look at her arms. They were riddled with little red marks.

"Why did you do it, Natalia? How could you be so stupid?"

"I couldn't go on living at the hotel, you see. I wanted to have a real baby, and I didn't dare ask you."

"Ask me?"

"Yes."

"I don't understand... You mean to say you wanted to have a baby... with me?"

"Yes."

"That's crazy..."

"It's the only thing that's going to save me."

"But Natalia..."

"If you don't help me, I'm going to drown myself in the fountain. Right now."

The old wry smile was about to appear on Frankie's lips.

"Let's go and get a coffee, Natalia."

"I don't want coffee, I want a fix!" she yelled.

Frankie managed to stay calm.

"Look, Natalia, what you need is something to eat and a bit of rest. The only thing I can do is take you for breakfast, or take you to the hospital. There's no way I'm going to give you money so that you can go on killing yourself. All right?"

Natalia shuddered. She began to shake. She was in a bad way.

"And are we going to have a baby, Antonio?" she asked, in a childlike voice.

"We can talk about that when you're in a better state."

"We could make a baby now."

"No."

"You just don't love me, because you know that I'm going to die."

"That'll do, Natalia. Are you coming with me, or not?"

"Wait."

She stepped aside, took off her glasses and smashed them on the ground. Then she stooped to pick up a long sliver of glass.

"You see this, Antonio?"

Frankie got to his feet.

"What are you doing, Natalia?" he asked, suddenly alarmed.

She took a step back.

"I'm going to slash my face."

"You're crazy..."

"Tell me you're going to help me."

Natalia slowly brought the piece of glass closer to her cheek. He could see the desperation in her squinty eyes.

Frankie tried to move closer to her.

"Don't move, Antonio."

"Stop that. Please!"

"I'm going to do it. Right now."

"I'm telling you, Natalia... Don't do it."

She smiled in a strange kind of way.

"I don't care any more, see."

Frankie hesitated for a moment or two. With the back of his hand he mopped away the sweat which had begun to gather on his brow. Finally he plucked up courage and said, "Go on then."

With a single rapid movement, Natalia pressed the glass against the side of her face and brought it down towards her jaw. At first it just traced a thin, red pencil-line. But then the blood began to flow.

"Natalia!"

Frankie took his handkerchief out of his pocket and dabbed at her cheek. Natalia was crying again. He had to do something.

"It hurts, Antonio."

He had to think fast. He thought it could be tricky to take Natalia to hospital looking the way she did, with her arms full of needle marks, barefoot and with a cut down the side of her face.

He decided to haul her off to Calle Fernando to look for an open chemist's. It wouldn't be easy at that time of day.

"I'm sorry, Antonio," she said, over and over again.

Luckily, just a few yards ahead there was the flashing red-cross sign of a chemist's shop.

"Wait here for me, Natalia. Don't move."

"Don't leave me alone, please..."

"Stay there, I'll only be a minute."

"Antonio!"

Frankie crossed the street, went into the chemist's and bought disinfectant, bandages and an antibiotic powder for the cut. He went back to fetch her, hailed a cab and took her off to the hotel.

"This is the last thing I'll be doing for you, Natalia," he told her, as they went up the dimly-lit hotel stairs. "The last fucking thing."

As Frankie opened the door, his eyes lighted on a woman the size of a tank. She was sitting at the reception desk with a bottle of muscatel and a box of biscuits at her elbow.

She looked like a ton of soft, beaten egg-white. She gave him a curious look as she held a glass in one hand and slowly chewed on a biscuit.

Her head was adorned with a perm made up of scores of tiny, tight, pinky-white curls. She had a face the size of a bus tyre and the pendulous cheeks of a bulldog. She was draped in a black dressing gown that would have hidden an average-sized dinosaur, and her feet were encased in a pair of red slippers. She was about sixty years old.

She looked down her nose at Frankie and asked:

"Hello! Who are you?"

For a moment, Frankie thought he might be in the wrong place, but it was obvious from the hotel key-board that he wasn't.

"I'm Antonio, the night porter."

The woman smiled and held out her hand.

"And I am Senorita Clementina, the sister of Senor Flores, may he rest in peace. How do you do?"

"Fine, thanks," Frankie replied, as he shook her hand.

At that moment the enormous woman clapped eyes on Natalia.

"Oh, the poor child! What's happened to her?"

"Well... she had an accident... she's a friend of mine, you see... I was going to see to her cut... I've bought this stuff."

Natalia started crying again.

Senorita Clementina got up from her seat, slowly and majestically, like a submarine coming up from the bottom of the sea.

"Let me have a look, Antonio," she said, and she removed Frankie's handkerchief from Natalia's face.

She examined the cut for a second or two. Then she took another swig of her muscatel, and finally pronounced:

"It's not serious."

"Are you sure?" Frankie asked.

"Sure. Give me some antiseptic."

Frankie unwrapped the packet they'd given him at the chemist's, and handed her the plasters.

"No, Antonio, the antiseptic..."

Frankie handed over the antibiotic powder.

"Forget it," the woman said. "You're useless. Why don't you sit and read a magazine or something. I'll see to her myself, thank you."

"I'm sorry," said Frankie, apologetically.

In no time at all, Senorita Clementina had seen to Natalia's cut.

"There you are," she said simply. "Now, what are you thinking of doing with her?"

"I've got nowhere to go," said Natalia, in a flash.

Frankie was beginning to feel alarmed.

"You can stay here, child," Senorita Clementina declared.

Natalia squeezed Frankie's hand.

"Will you let me stay in your room, Antonio?"

"Of course he will, child," Senorita Clementina intervened. "It's the only room free."

"Senorita Clementina... " Frankie began to say.

"Don't worry, Antonio. You two can be together, and I won't interfere."

"Fine, fine..."

"By the way, Antonio..."

"Yes?"

"I meant to tell you. As from today, I'm in charge of the hotel. I'll be living in. It'll give me a bit of company."

"I'm very happy to hear it, Senorita Clementina."

"Now, you didn't come in to work last night, did you?"

Frankie lowered his eyes.

"Well you see, I had a..."

"It doesn't matter. Go and get some rest."

"All right, Senorita Clementina. See you later," Frankie said as he headed off down the corridor, followed by Natalia.

"Antonio!" the woman called after him.

"What?"

"You know what? You're the spitting image of Frank Sinatra. I think I'll call you Frankie from now on."

"Feel free. Everyone else does."

Alone with Natalia in his little room, Frankie moved

around cautiously, trying to avoid physical contact. She sat on the bed and shed her tattered shirt. They sat like that for a while. Frankie didn't budge from the only chair in the room.

"What are you going to do, Antonio?" Natalia asked.

"Nothing."

"Don't you want to lie down?"

"No."

Natalia got up and took off her trousers. She had no knickers on. She stood there completely naked. She turned to Frankie.

"I did all this just to be with you, Antonio."

"And you succeeded."

Natalia lay down on the bed and covered herself with the sheet.

"I'm cold. All my bones are aching."

"So what am I supposed to do?"

"Come and lie down next to me. Please."

Frankie lay down next to her. Fully dressed. He didn't even take off his shoes. Natalia pressed up against him.

"I've just spent the night with a woman, Natalia."

"I don't care."

"Well, that's a start."

"What's the matter with you, Antonio."

"I don't know. It feels like something's gone, inside my head. For ever."

Frankie reached out his hand to the bedside table, took his cigarettes and a lighter, lit up a Ducados and sat there staring at the patchy, damp ceiling of his room. He was falling asleep.

He dozed off. Until the moment that Natalia suddenly flung the sheet in the air, hurled herself on his body, seized him by the hair and started kissing him frantically on the mouth.

"We're going to have one now, Antonio, you'll see..."

By the time Frankie had opened his eyes, his shirt was

already unbuttoned and Natalia was licking his chest and struggling to undo the buttons of his fly.

"Have one what?! Stop it, Natalia... You gone mad or something?"

"We're going to have a baby, silly," she said, working hard.

"Wait, please... wait... Stop it!"

He tried to hold her down by one wrist, but she bit his hand and carried on struggling with his trousers. A moment later, she'd managed to get them down to his knees.

"You can't get away now," she said, in a husky voice.

For a moment Frankie stared at her face.

She looked like some demented fairy, with dishevelled hair, an enormous sticking plaster on one cheek and eyes that were hell-bent on mutual destruction. Her ribs stood out like ridges under her yellow skin, and she moved like a crazed hyena baying at the moon.

His face was soaked with Natalia's saliva. He couldn't get her off him. She was beginning to hurt him. He began to feel that he was going to have to be cruel with her.

"We're going to do it, we're going to do it!" she said triumphantly, as she felt Frankie put his arm round her little waist, penetrate her, and at the same time stick half his index finger up her bum. Natalia was completely encrusted onto his body. Frankie barely even had to move. She was doing it all. She had the irritating habit of biting. The bed was about to fall apart. It was making a terrible noise. It wasn't used to having people screwing on it. Frankie remembered the bad old days, how he used to masturbate in the mornings when he woke up, or lusted painfully after women on bar-stools. Things seemed to have changed.

They were lying there, panting and motionless, when there was suddenly the sound of Senorita Clementina knocking at the door.

"Frankie!"

"Yes?"

"The postman's here. He wants you to sign for something. I think it's a telegram."

Frankie sat up in bed.

"I'm fucked!" he muttered.

"What shall I tell him?" she asked.

"Nothing. I'm coming."

"OK."

"Don't be long, Antonio," Natalia said.

"All right."

Frankie put on his trousers and went out into the corridor. Senorita Clementina was sitting in reception. She'd finished her box of biscuits and had a new bottle of muscatel on the table. The postman was standing next to her, looking bored.

"Are you Antonio Castro Fernandez?" he asked.

Frankie nodded.

"Sign here, please."

He held out a kind of notepad, and pointed to the bottom of the page as he handed him a pen.

Frankie signed. The postman handed over the telegram, said goodbye, and left.

"I've always liked telegrams," said Senorita Clementina. "They're a bit like Russian roulette."

"Well, it's hardly going to be good news, is it."

"Why not? Maybe they're offering you a job as a double for Sinatra. I love the movies, you know. My favourite hobby's collecting photos of film stars. I've got albums full of them. If you like, I'll show them to you one day."

"Fine, fine," Frankie answered, a touch impatiently.

"D'you fancy a little drink with me?"

"Not right now, thanks. I'm a bit nervous about that telegram."

"Open it then."

"I don't think I dare, for the moment."

"But I'm dying to know what's in it, Frankie."

"I'm sorry."

Senorita Clementina took another swig at the muscatel, a quizzical look on her enormous face.

"Hey, what's happened to your neck? Looks like the vampires have been having a go at you."

"Oh, I don't know... It must have been..."

"Forget it. I'll see you later."

"OK," said Frankie, and he disappeared off to his room.

Natalia was kneeling on the bed. Her two hands were resting on her stomach, and there was a look of ecstasy in her eyes. She didn't seem to be bothered by the cold any more, and she didn't seem to be in pain either.

"Oh, Antonio!" she said, in a dreamy voice. "It moved, it moved..."

Frankie looked at her, puzzled.

"Moved? What moved?"

"Our baby, Frankie. It's kicking in my tummy."

"You don't say!"

"What shall we call it?"

"I don't know, Natalia."

"Of course, I'm really hoping it'll be a girl, you know."

"Please, Natalia. Will you try and get some sleep. I need a bit of peace and quiet, all right?! PEACE AND QUIET!"

Natalia frowned like an angry child, lay down and covered herself with the sheet.

"Aren't you coming to bed, Antonio?"

"When you're asleep."

Natalia promptly rolled over in bed with her face to the wall, stuck one arm under the pillow, shut her eyes, and pretended to sleep.

Frankie waited for a minute or two, went for a piss, came back, sat on the chair and opened the telegram. It read:

ANTONIO: WILL YOU MARRY ME? HORTENSIA

9

Camacho the barber arranged himself more comfortably at the bar counter, lit a fresh cigarette from the stub of his previous one, and said:
"Frankie, I've been listening to you for the past two hours, and I can't think of anything to suggest. I'm sorry. What can I say?"

"Don't worry. I suppose everything'll sort itself out."

"I'll tell you what, Frankie."

"What?"

"Why don't you go and talk with Contreras?"

"Contreras?"

"Yes, he begs on the corner of Hospital and Egipciacas. He has a sort of stand there. You must have seen him."

"Sure, I know the one."

"Anyway, he sits there on the steps, with a bottle of wine and a Barcelona FC banner, a candle, and replicas of a couple of saints, and people throw him coins. He just sits there — he doesn't actually do anything."

"And why do you think I should talk to him?"

"Well, he's mad as a hatter, but sometimes people go to ask him things, and he gives them answers. It's usually the first thing that pops into his head, but, you never know, it might give you an idea."

Frankie shrugged his shoulders.

"I've got nothing to lose."

"What's more," Camacho continued, "he's got a pair of lady friends, or lovers, I'm not sure which. Two old ruins who hang out with him, and bring him wine and cigarettes. Sometimes they spend hours together. He's like their pimp, you see. One time he's with one of them, then the other one turns up, and they all sit and drink wine together. Anyway, usually he's on his own. You can talk with him and tell him all your problems. For a hundred pesetas you can bore the pants off him all night."

Frankie looked at his watch. "I'm supposed to be at work in the hotel in half an hour."

"You've got time. Tell him I sent you."

"Camacho."

"What?"

"You don't think I'll be making an idiot of myself?"

"I doubt that it'd be the first time."

"That's for sure."

"Well, then... ?"

Contreras was sitting as usual on a doorstep, at the corner of the street. This was his spot, and nobody could shift him from it.

He looked like one of the three wise kings, fallen on hard times. He had long grey hair, tied behind with a rubber band, thick lips and a ruddy, puffy face. In one hand, he held a bottle of wine.

He was counting the money at his feet. He seemed to have not a care in the world. He was wearing a T-shirt which had a picture of the front page of the *Sun*, with a headline that read: "SID VICIOUS IS DEAD!"

Frankie went over to him. He hadn't the first idea what to say. In fact he was on the point of turning back.

Finally he plucked up courage and said: "Are you Contreras? I wanted to talk to you for a minute. Camacho sent me."

Contreras sat, impassively, counting his money. When he'd finished, he said:

"You'll have to pay in advance."

Frankie gave him five hundred pesetas. For the moment,

his bingo win was paying for everything.

"Women. Must be women," Contreras muttered, as he took the banknote, put it in one of his pockets and began dismantling his side-show. His night was made.

He loaded all his bits and pieces into a little handcart, greased his hand back over his hair, and returned to sit on the steps.

"Well?" he finally asked, with a look of boredom. Frankie was stuck for words.

"It's to do with women, isn't it?" Contreras repeated.

"How do you know?"

"Simple enough. It's only when a bloke's in a mess with a woman that he's going to come and blow five hundred pesetas with the likes of me."

Frankie sank back into a brooding silence.

"If you're not going to say anything, I'm off."

"Will you give me a drink?"

Contreras clicked his tongue and reluctantly passed him the bottle. Frankie took a swig, and continued:

"Well there's a forty-five year-old widow, and she wants to marry me. She's got a crazy son who wants to kill me. What should I do?"

"She got any dough?"

"Not a lot."

"Dump her."

"What's more," Frankie continued, "I've got a bit involved with this sixteen-year-old kid, but she's on heroin and, well, she's a bit gone in the head. She wants to have a baby with me, you see..."

Contreras gave a prolonged yawn.

"She'll drive you nuts too. Dump her."

"You could be right, Contreras."

"Anything else?"

"Well, a few days ago I picked up a prostitute in a bingo hall. At the start she had me blowing lots of money, but when it came to bedtime, she decided she wasn't going to charge me. I've got her phone number. She's dynamite."

"Go for it," Contreras pronounced.

"Maybe I'll call her tonight, or in the morning. Some time, anyway."

"Now can I ask you a question?"

"Sure," Frankie replied.

"How old are you?"

"Forty."

"*And you still take women seriously? You must be crazy!*"

Frankie gritted his teeth and lowered his eyes.

"I can't help it."

"Of course you can."

All of a sudden, without knowing why, Frankie said:

"You know, there's a midget who writes me poems. She's twenty-two years old, blonde, and she's got blue eyes..."

Contreras's gloomy face suddenly lit up.

"A dwarf?" he asked, enthusiastically.

"Yes."

"Now that's something else."

"Do you think so?"

"Sure. A nice young midget, blonde, with a tight pussy. I had one once. She was too much!"

"You're kidding..."

"They're no trouble, they don't bug you. They don't crowd your space. Everybody passes them over, but it doesn't worry them. They look at life from below, and have a very different take on it. How can I explain. They have more worldly wisdom. They're more real than other women."

"She's only three foot four, Contreras..."

"Now I *know* you understand nothing... !"

Frankie smiled his wry smile.

"In other words, you know everything, and I'm supposed to take up with the midget?"

"Exactly."

"Don't fuck about, Contreras..."

"It's your funeral, pal, your funeral..."

By now Frankie was smiling again. He got up from the doorway where they'd been sitting, gave Contreras a friendly wink, walked a few steps, crossed the street and went into the hotel.

There was nobody in his chair.

He went to the kitchen, put some water on for a coffee, went back to his desk, turned on the radio and glanced up at the key-board.

There was no sign of Natalia. She'd already left him twice, for ever, and been back at the hotel within a couple of hours. At this moment she was probably out in the street. And he couldn't be bothered to go out looking for her.

Frankie looked in the drawer for Isabel's phone number. He was sure he'd left it there. He hunted through his clothes, and then searched his room. The bloody number had disappeared. He could always find her at the bingo hall again. But he didn't want to turn up there without having talked with her first. What's more, he couldn't remember for the life of him whether he'd given her the hotel's number.

He sat down at the desk with the cup of coffee in his hand, and tried to forget Isabel. He wondered what it would be like going to bed with a blonde midget.

Somebody rang at the door, and Frankie went to answer.

The man at the door looked like a seedy Puerto Rican straight out of a third-rate TV mini-series. He had lank black hair that had been moistened and combed straight back, triangular sideburns, and a thin moustache. His face was a sort of mothy colour. He leaned on the doorframe with one hand. He had his other hand in the back pocket of his jeans. The weight of his body was on his left leg, and his right leg was bent at the knee. He looked as if he was chewing, or pretending to chew, gum. He had a grin on his face.

"How goes, lover-boy?" he said. "I'm Juan Cuevas Heredia."

"Who?" Frankie asked.

"From the club, fellow member! You mean you don't remember me?"

Frankie remembered at once. The armed robber who'd spent five years in Carabanchel... here, on his doorstep!

"Sure, come on in," said Frankie, gesturing impotently and at the same time cursing the cruel and unfeeling stars that were playing with his fate.

Juan Cuevas Heredia stayed where he was. The only thing that moved was his jaw, which was working overtime. He was pounding the gum to pieces.

"You sure it's cool?" he asked.

Frankie shook his head, uncomprehendingly.

"What d'you mean."

"I mean, you're not worried about getting involved with the likes of me...?"

"Well, it depends..."

"You can call me Juan, OK?"

"All right."

Frankie led him into reception. Juan Cuevas Heredia passed slowly through the door. He eyed the fading wallpaper, the dingy key-board and the lone armchair.

"Are you thinking of staying here?" Frankie asked, a touch anxiously.

A strange head, like that of the Loch Ness Monster, emerged from the depths of the corridor.

"Hey, Frankie. Do you fancy a quick drink?"

Senorita Clementina erupted on the scene, enveloped in her black dressing gown.

"Er... Well... a guest has just arrived."

Juan Cuevas Heredia and Senorita Clementina gazed at each other.

She stuck out her chest, re-positioned her breasts, raised her bottle of muscatel a few inches, smiled like a young girl, and said:

"Cheers!"

He left off chewing his gum and gazed at her in disbelief for several long seconds. Then something prompted him to move his shoulders a bit and bow slightly. He smiled, showing a row of ailing, yellow teeth.

"My name's Juan. How's tricks?" he said, by way of greeting.

"This is Senorita Clementina. She owns the hotel," Frankie said hurriedly.

"We could give him room 4," she suggested.

"But we don't know if he even wants to stay, Senorita Clementina."

"I think he does. Don't you, Juan?"

Juan casually put his hand into the right pocket of his jeans, took out some green notes and flashed them like a conjuror who's just pulled off his best trick.

"Money is no problem."

Senorita Clementina was in there like a shot. "Come on," she said, "I'll show you to your room."

She came over to Juan, latched onto his arm and hauled him off to the darkest depths of the boarding house. Frankie settled into his chair and shut his eyes. All he wanted was a bit of peace and quiet. He just wanted to sit there, letting the night pass, slowly and silently, like some ancient bus crossing the white face of the moon. All he could do was wait.

Ten minutes went by, and Senorita Clementina had still not returned to reception. Juan neither.

"There's going to be a right carry-on here," thought Frankie, and he dozed off. He slept until the ring of the phone woke him.

"Hello," said Frankie, sleepily.

"Excuse me. I'd like to talk with Senor Antonio."

It sounded like a woman's voice.

"That's me. Who's speaking?"

"Thank goodness I've found you, honey. It's Rosita."

Frankie leapt up from his chair. More people from the bloody club!

"I was asleep, Rosita."

"I'm sorry, dear boy, but I was feeling so lonely. That's why I thought of phoning you. My mum's died. I'm never going to see her again. Have you any idea how that feels? I'm desperate. I've got to talk to somebody, so that I can tell them what's happening with me, because the pain in my heart is so terrible, I can't stand it, angel, I really can't stand it.

"I'm sorry."

"And that's not all. A few days ago, Ramon left the bar, and now I've got nobody. I'm a pitiful wretch, Antonio. Life has treated me very cruelly. Last night I almost decided to drink a bottle of bleach, and go and join my saintly mother in heaven."

"I don't know what to say."

"I want to ask you something, Antonio, because you're good as gold, and you're going to help me."

"What?"

"Would you let me come and see you at the hotel, and have a drink with you?"

"I'm working, Rosita."

"Please, Antonio, for the love of God, let me come."

Rosita seemed to be crying. Frankie never could stand the sound of women crying. He was going to have to learn.

"Can't it wait until tomorrow?"

"I'll die, Antonio, I swear it. On my mother's memory."

Frankie paused for a long while, angrily stubbed out his cigarette in the metal ashtray, and then said:

"Oh, all right."

"Thanks, angel. I knew you'd say yes. I'll be round in five minutes. Goodbye, honey."

Frankie decided that he needed a drink. He had a bottle of whiskey in his room. The bingo win was still paying for his drinks. He went to fetch the bottle and poured himself half a glass. He was beginning to feel better. He had to think things out calmly. The whiskey helped relieve the tension. These people from the club were beginning to strangle him, like a rope tightening around his neck. The idea of writing to the blonde midget suddenly seemed ridiculous. He couldn't explain the reasons that were driving him to it. Everything would get even more complicated. He imagined Begonia turning up at the hotel with a little suitcase in her hand. The whole membership of the lonely hearts club would arrive on his doorstep. He'd go out of his mind.

Senora Hortensia might turn up any minute, dressed in a wedding dress. Rosita was on her way, and Juan Cuevas was already there.

He poured himself another whiskey.

"Hi, Frankie."

Manolo stood there, wearing a green jacket, custard-coloured trousers, a black shirt and a silver tie. He reeked of cheap cologne. For sure he was going out whoring.

"What's new, Manolo?"

"A chick rang for you this afternoon."

Frankie almost dropped his glass.

"Did she leave her name?"

"Isabel."

"Did she leave a message?"

"She said she'd call again."

"OK. Fancy a whiskey?"

"Don't mind if I do," said Manolo, pleasantly surprised.

Frankie poured him a whiskey.

"I bet you don't know where I'm going," Manolo said, with a broad wink.

"You're going out screwing," Frankie answered, without pausing for thought.

Manolo looked at him in surprise.

"How did you guess?"

Frankie shrugged his shoulders.

"Intuition..."

"OK, pal, I must be off," said Manolo, finishing his whiskey.

"See you later."

Frankie took the newspaper and turned to the crossword. Crossword puzzles seemed to clear his brain. He solved a few clues. By the time he got to 8 down, he had a notion that the words had changed:

```
        H
  R O S I T A
    R
    T         N
  B E G O N I A
    N         T
    S         A
    I         L
  J U A N     I
        I S A B E L
```

He promptly put the newspaper aside and concentrated on the whiskey. Then the doorbell rang.

Rosita was not wearing her wig, but was displaying a large pink bald head. She was dressed as she'd been dressed on the day that Frankie first met her. But her perfume was different. This time she smelled of vanilla essence.

"Thanks for letting me come, kid," she said by way of greeting. "I've brought you a present."

Frankie sat her down in the rickety old armchair.

"Ten minutes, Rosita. I told you, I'm working..."

Frankie poured her a small whiskey.

"You're so generous, Antonio. God will reward you."

Rosita dispatched the whiskey in one gulp, and with a

purple handkerchief mopped the beads of sweat that were showing on her bald head.

"You've no idea how much I'm suffering, honey. I've no one left to turn to. I'm completely alone in the world."

"You'll find someone."

"Do you like me, Antonio?"

"What can I say... ?"

"Please, say yes."

Frankie shrugged his shoulders, and slowly the wry smile returned to his lips.

"OK. Yes."

Rosita shut her eyes, and leaned back in the armchair.

"Say it again, Antonio," she whispered.

"Yes, fuck it! Yes!" Frankie yelled.

"I'm sorry, honey, I didn't mean to upset you."

"That's all right."

"Oh, I almost forgot to give you your present," said Rosita, opening her white plastic handbag. "I'm sure you're going to like it."

"What is it," Frankie asked, intrigued.

"Wait a second, angel," she said, as she searched for something in the bottom of her bag. Finally she pulled out something that looked like a small ball of yellow cotton-wool.

"Look at him, Antonio. Isn't he lovely?"

Frankie went over to Rosita to take a closer look at what she had in her hand.

"It's a chicken," he said, with a note of alarm.

"A chick, dear. Take him. He's yours," she said, and she handed the creature over.

"I don't know anything about chickens."

"I find them enchanting. I've got lots more at home."

"What am I supposed to do with a chicken?"

"Well, you can feed it.. and you can play with it..."

"I told you, I can't."

"Please, Antonio, you should never turn down a

present. Look, poor thing, it's started to chirp."

Frankie left the chick sitting on the table, took the bottle and poured himself another whiskey.

"Look, Rosita, try to understand," said Frankie, making a great effort to keep calm. "I'm very grateful that you've given me this chicken, but I don't *want* a chicken. Is that clear?"

"But you could keep him in your room. He could be your friend."

"*I don't want this fucking chicken!*"

"But the poor thing hasn't done you any harm."

"Right, Rosita. That's enough," said Frankie. He looked at the clock. "I've got things to do now."

"All right, I'm leaving."

"Fine. I'll come with you. I've got to buy some cigarettes anyway."

Frankie left Rosita at the hotel door, crossed the street and bought a packet of Ducados in the bar opposite. At last he was beginning to unwind.

The first thing he saw when he got back to the hotel was the chicken, which was still on the desk in reception. Chirping.

10

The colouring of the sore was red and yellow. It was covered by a thin layer which looked like plastic. It was about the size of a lentil, but a bit more elongated. It must have contained thousands of lethal microbes. It looked imposing and terrifying. It was the new and heinous king of Frankie's cock.

"It could only have been Natalia or Isabel," he thought as he turned the shower off.

Frankie began to dry himself, extremely carefully. He'd only just discovered the sore. He felt fear welling up inside him. This was the first time anything like this had happened to him. He didn't have the faintest idea of what to expect next.

For a moment he had a mental vision of his body becoming full of horrible sores. Ulcers in his mouth, followed by madness, and, finally, death.

He emerged from the bathroom with a towel round his waist. Manolo was reading a magazine in reception. There was nobody else in sight.

"Hey, Manolo."

"What?" he said, not bothering to raise his eyes.

"I'm screwed."

Manolo looked up.

"God, Frankie! You've gone as white as a sheet."

"I've got reason to be."

"Too much whiskey?"

"Syphilis."

Manolo backed off in an attempt to distance himself from Frankie:

"You'd better get along to the hospital. Bits of your cock might start dropping off otherwise."

"Thanks a lot, Manolo!"

"You got no idea who it was?"

"Two chicks. Must have been one or the other."

"Fucking whores."

"Has Natalia been back?"

"Not as far as I know."

"OK. I'll get dressed and go down to the hospital."

"Hang on, Frankie. I think there was something for you."

Manolo took a number of letters that were lying on the table, picked one out, and handed it to Frankie.

"Here you are."

"That's all I need," said Frankie, and went off to his room.

On this occasion he couldn't resist reading the letter straight away. He lit a cigarette, stretched out on the bed, and slit open the envelope.

Brother Antonio:

Yesterday I talked with Jesus. He told me that you are the Wicked One.

As you can imagine, I am obliged to tell you that your only chance of salvation lies in absolute repentance of your sins, and in saying twenty hours of prayer every day. In addition, you must drink a litre of holy water before you go to bed, and another when you get up. It is also imperative that you place as many lighted candles as possible by your bedside.

I expect that some horrible sign of the Devil has appeared on your body. A sign of evil, probably in the form of some horrible and incurable disease.

The Virgin Mary is still crying warm tears, and I am ready to make the greatest of sacrifices in order to help her to regain her peace of mind.

I hope that you will write to me as soon as possible to say that you are willing to drive the Wicked One out of your body. In that case, you can count on my assistance. If you do not agree, I shall be obliged to bring your evil life to an end.

Brother Blanco Sol.

Frankie tore the letter into shreds. This was the first death threat that he'd received from a member of the club, and he imagined that it probably wouldn't be the last. When he got back from hospital, he'd write to the club, telling them to remove his name from their fucking brochure.

He'd had enough of them.

He got up from the bed, dressed, and went down to reception.

Senorita Clementina was sitting in the armchair. She had the chick in her hands, and was giving it little kisses on its beak.

"Look what I've found, Frankie. Isn't he adorable?"

"If you say so..."

"I'm going to call him Cheep-Cheep. What do you think?"

"Sounds fair enough."

"By the way, Juan said he wants to talk to you. He's waiting in the bar next door."

"OK, I'll drop in."

Juan Cuevas Heredia was devouring an enormous potato tortilla. On the table was a plate of salad, a bottle of wine and a loaf of bread. He looked starving. When he saw Frankie he waved with his fork to indicate that he should sit down.

"I'm knackered, pal," was the first thing he said. "That Clementina goes a bit!"

"What happened?"

"I got it on with her last night."

"You're kidding!"

Juan gave him a knowing look.

"You don't believe me?"

"Yes, sure, I believe you."

"Do you fancy a bite to eat?"

"I'm not hungry."

"You're a real arsehole," said Juan slowly. It's obvious what's wrong with you. Some doll's put you off your food. I can see it in your face."

"That's my business."

"You're one of those types who thinks more than is good for them."

"Maybe."

"What you need is something to cheer you up. How d'you fancy going out on a binge tonight?"

"I'm not feeling too good, Juan. In fact I'm just on my way to hospital..."

"What's the matter with you?"

"The clap, or something. I don't really know."

"Women again..."

"What's more, I'm thinking of taking up with a midget."

Juan shook his head.

"You're in a hole, pal. You're thinking the only thing that's going to get you out is a woman. But you've got to do it yourself, for fuck's sake. If not, things will go from bad to worse."

Frankie looked at the clock and got up from the table.

"I'm off, Juan. I'll see you later."

Frankie came out of the hospital with several million units of penicillin floating around in his body. He felt weak, and he needed a drink, but alcohol wasn't allowed during the treatment. He didn't want to see anybody, and the last thing he wanted was a night out with Juan. When he got back to the hotel, he locked himself in his room. At a certain point the image of the as-yet-unknown Begonia

Montana floated before his eyes, and prompted him to sit down and write:

Dear Begonia,
This is the last letter I'm writing before I resign from the club. They're all driving me crazy. I've had everything from proposals of marriage to death threats.

It's only now that I feel able to get in touch with you, to find out more about you and try to understand you.

I'm an average sort of person who just wants to live a quiet life, and, if possible, share it with somebody else.

This doesn't seem too much to ask, but I'm finding it as hard as wiggling my ears or flying like Superman.

I don't know if you and I will end up being friends, but I'd like to give it a go anyway. You never know, do you?

I liked your poem a lot, even though I don't know a lot about poetry. Thanks for sending it.

I could tell you a lot more, but I'd be here all day.

Anyway, Begonia, you know where to find me. You can count on me.
Antonio.

Frankie read the letter through several times before deciding to put it in an envelope and stick a stamp on. In an obscure, confused kind of way, he was hoping for something from Begonia Montana.

A few minutes before he was due to start work, he went out into the street, posted the letter, and then returned to the hotel.

Juan and Senorita Clementina were waiting for him.

"So, you two are going out to enjoy yourselves tonight?" she said, as she saw him returning.

"I don't know, I really ought to..."

"Don't worry," Juan interrupted. "It's all been arranged."

"I'll do the night shift, Frankie," said Senorita Clementina.

"What did you call him?" asked Juan, smiling.

"Frankie. After Frank Sinatra. Can't you see? He's the spitting image."

"So you're a singer, pal..."

"That's just what people call me."

"Have you got enough money?" Senorita Clementina asked, like a mother sending her kids to the pictures.

At that moment the phone rang. She answered it.

"Frankie, it's for you," she said in a low voice.

"Who is it?" Frankie asked her, nervously.

"It's a girl... Isabel."

She handed him the phone and nodded Juan in the direction of the corridor.

"We'll leave him alone," she ordered.

"Hello, Isabel?"

"Antonio, I want to ask you something."

Her voice was sharp as a razor.

"What?"

"I've been infected. I need to know if it was you."

Frankie passed his hand gingerly over his forehead as if he were touching an open cut.

"Look, kid, this afternoon I was down at the hospital. I've caught it too, but I promise you, before I slept with you, I hadn't touched a woman in more than a year."

"That's what they all say."

"Please, Isabel, there's no reason why I should lie to you."

"I wish I could see you face to face, Antonio. It's easier to trick people over the phone."

"If you saw my face, you'd cry."

"Don't try to be funny. This thing is more serious than you seem to think."

"Mightn't it have been another... client?" Frankie asked, timidly.

"Impossible. It's been a long while since the last time."

"How long?"

"I don't know, a month or so... Anyway, I had a check-up a couple of days before I slept with you, and there was nothing wrong with me."

"You'll have to believe me, Isabel. I don't know how I can prove it to you."

She paused for a moment.

"It must have been that son of a bitch Camilo. I'm sick of him," she said, in a hoarse voice.

"And who's Camilo?"

"My friend. We live together."

"I see."

"I'll talk to him tonight. I should kick him out. I can't stand him any more."

"Take it easy, kid."

"You know what it is, Antonio? I need to believe in someone. I want to trust someone, but somehow I never seem to manage it."

"You're too attractive, Isabel, that's your problem."

"I don't know. You're ugly enough and you're still pretty untogether."

"Do you mean that?"

"It was a joke, silly."

"I'm glad to hear it."

"Tell you what, why don't you call round at the bingo hall and we can go for a drink."

"I'm not supposed to touch alcohol."

Isabel laughed.

"That's a point, neither am I..."

"If you like, we could go for a Coke."

"Actually, thinking about it, tomorrow might be better. I hope you understand."

"Sure."

"I'll ring you."

"OK."

"Kisses to you, Antonio."

"And kisses to you too, kid."

Frankie smiled.

For a moment he felt like climbing up on the table and singing a song, or leaping about like he'd scored the winning goal in the dying seconds of a football match. Instead he just sat there quietly, with an amazed and idiotic smile on his face, staring at the phone.

Senorita Clementina returned to reception.

"What's up, Frankie? You look like you're drunk. You haven't fallen in love, have you?"

"I think I have."

"You've blown it, pal," said Juan as he appeared down the corridor. "That's the worst thing that can happen to a man."

Frankie couldn't stop smiling. He started playing with the buttons on his shirt.

"I'm sure that she needs me," he said, to himself. "It's amazing."

"You're going to end up with no buttons left," said Senorita Clementina. "Look, you've pulled one off already."

"I think I'm going out on my own. I don't think I can put up with him all night, the way he's carrying on," said Juan.

"We could all stay in and play cards," suggested Senorita Clementina.

"Count me out," said Juan swiftly.

Frankie came down to earth again.

"Look, Juan, I'm sorry. I'm not feeling too well. Anyway, I can't touch alcohol at the moment. Maybe we'd best leave it for another night."

Juan turned to Senorita Clementina and shook his head.

"What did I tell you, eh? What a rat... !"

Frankie smiled again.

"Well go screw yourself then," said Juan. He spat out

his toothpick, took his jacket, and went out, slamming the door.

"Look, Frankie, if you're not feeling well, I could stand in for you tonight."

"No, really, don't worry..."

"It's all the same to me. Anyway, I won't be able to sleep till Juan gets back. What's more, I've finished my muscatel."

"Do you want me to go down to the bar and get you a bottle?"

Senorita Clementina smiled.

"Good idea, and while you're gone I'll put some coffee on."

"Fine. I'll be back with the muscatel right away."

"Just a moment, Frankie."

"Yes?"

"I usually make my coffee on the strong side. Is that all right with you?"

"As you like, Isabel."

The sea was as blue as a young girl's eyes. A light spray crowned the wave-tops and a seagull hovered over the rocks. A red and white fishing boat was beached on the sand. The sun was like a bejewelled emperor, shedding its light on all things.

Frankie turned the postcard over, saw that it was from Natalia:

Dear Antonio,
I'm in Formentera, and I'm thinking of staying here until our baby is born. I've got a friend here who's teaching me to play the flute, and she's given me a sleeping bag.
I go swimming with no clothes on, and at night I write your name in the sand.
Natalia.

"She would have been a big mistake," Frankie murmured to himself. He took another look at the postcard and at that moment realized that Natalia might *really* be pregnant.

Frankie was of the opinion that having a baby would be one way of changing his life, but with Natalia as the mother, he'd without doubt have ended his days in a nuthouse.

They'd probably have ended up with a kid that was green-skinned and insane — a murderer, who drank Coke with absinthe and who, one winter's night, would blow

up his bed with nitroglycerine. Natalia would feed him
on dead rats, and would play the flute to get him off to
sleep. For his birthday, she would give him a plastic
syringe and half a gramme of pure heroin.

Frankie left the postcard on the hotel desk, hung his
key on the board, and went off to eat.

He sat at the counter, ordered two fried eggs with
sausage and a sliced tomato, a bottle of non-carbonated
mineral water and a slice of bread. He settled himself more
comfortably on the bar stool, because his buttocks were
hurting him on account of the injections, and he waited
for the food. As he was about to dunk a piece of bread in
his fried egg, he suddenly saw with absolute clarity the
face of Senora Hortensia in the egg yolk.

Frankie sat, paralyzed, with a piece of bread in his
fingers, gazing at her face. She seemed to be crying. One
after another, Senora Hortensia's tears rolled down her
cheeks. He got the impression that she was trying to tell
him something from the greasy depths of the fried egg, but
all she could do was express an unfathomable pain.

She was more than willing to be his wife; she was trying
to make him understand that she needed him at her side,
that she was offering him her life for better or for worse, and
that she loved him.

The waiter came over from behind the bar.

"What's up? Eggs no good?"

Frankie looked at him uncomprehendingly.

"What?"

"I said, are the eggs no good?"

"The eggs...?"

"Are they too runny for you?"

"No, they're fine, thanks..."

Frankie was worried that he would never again be able to
look at a fried egg without seeing the disconsolate face of
Senora Hortensia, who, by the way, he was unlikely ever to
see again.

He drank some water and decided that he'd tackle the second egg without looking at it, in case it too had Senora Hortensia's face. But he couldn't avoid looking.

In the other yolk, he saw Isabel taking her clothes off.

She did it like she was doing a screen-test for MGM. She was wearing a flesh-coloured bra and panties. Her French perfume overcame the smell of the fried egg, and it was as if she was about to leap from the round yellow screen at any moment.

"Isabel... " said Frankie, addressing the yoke.

The waiter shook his head, and clicked his tongue: "Are you sure you wouldn't rather try something else?"

At that moment Isabel's bra came flying towards Frankie.

"Excuse me. Are you feeling all right?" the waiter asked.

"Yes, thanks," Frankie answered, his eyes glued to the plate.

"They'll be cold soon," the waiter said.

Frankie had his nose half an inch away from the fried egg. Isabel was slowly sliding her hands down to her knickers.

"This guy's out to lunch," murmured the waiter, and he went off to attend to another customer.

The sound of twenty-five-peseta pieces tumbling into the tray of the bar's one-armed bandit, combined with the triumphant whoop of the lucky winner, shattered Frankie's vision.

The food was cold by now, and anyway he was no longer able to eat the eggs. He felt obliged to call the waiter over again.

"Excuse me, please," he said timidly.

The waiter gave him a dirty look.

"What do you want now?"

"Do you think you could change these for something else?"

"What are you — a bloody comedian?" exclaimed the

waiter, as he took the plate away.

An hour after Frankie had returned to the hotel, there was another phone call from Isabel.

"Antonio?"

"Yes, it's me."

"It's Isabel here. Do you think you could come round to my house tonight?"

Her voice sounded tense and fearful.

"I have to work tonight, but we could meet now, if you like, because I've still got a bit of time."

"No, I can't."

"The trouble is, kid..."

"Please, Antonio, please... I can't say any more. Say that you'll come."

Frankie hesitated for a moment.

"All right, I'll try to sort something out."

"The Florida Apartments, on Calle Caspe. First floor. I'll be expecting you at ten. Please, don't let me down."

"Isabel, can't you tell me the problem...?"

"I'm sorry, I've got to hang up. Goodbye."

Frankie put the phone down, went to his room, and, even though he was off alcohol, finished off the rest of the whiskey in his bottle.

He couldn't begin to imagine what Isabel's problem was. For a moment he thought of calling her back, but then he remembered he'd lost her number. Anyway, he had no way of knowing whether she'd been calling from her place. Dark thoughts began forming in his mind. It was six in the evening — four hours to go to ten o'clock. He would have to talk with Senorita Clementina.

He found her feeding Cheep-Cheep in reception.

"Senorita Clementina..."

"What's the matter, Frankie?"

"I'd like to ask you a favour."

"It's to do with the girl, isn't it?"

Frankie gave her a look of surprise.

"Yes, she called me just now. It sounds like she's got problems, and she wants me to go round."

"That's fine, Frankie."

"Thanks a lot."

"By the way, have you seen Juan?"

"No."

"He didn't come in last night. He's probably gone to rob a chemist's or something. I hope he's struck lucky."

Frankie gave one of his wry smiles and looked at his watch. He couldn't hang about. He had to find something to do.

"I'm off, Senorita Clementina," he said abruptly.

"As you like. I hope things sort themselves out."

"Thanks. Goodbye."

"Aren't you going to say goodbye to Cheep-Cheep?"

"Goodbye, Cheep-Cheep," he said, as he went out.

At a quarter to ten, Frankie took a cab to Isabel's.

He'd started sweating again. He opened the cab window and breathed in the humid air of the city. It didn't help much. He couldn't wait to get there. To be close to Isabel. To look into her eyes, to talk with her, to feel her arse, to smell her smell, to kiss her hair, to hear her laugh, to lick her tongue, to win her heart.

The cab finally arrived in front of a modern apartment block. Frankie paid the driver with a thousand-peseta note, didn't bother to wait for the change, and got out of the cab.

As he reached the entrance to the building, he saw the gilded letters of the sign that said: Florida Apartments.

Isabel obviously wasn't doing too badly for herself.

Frankie went up to the first floor and rang the doorbell. No answer. He lit a cigarette, waited a few seconds, and then rang again. There was no sign of Isabel. It was unthinkable that she would have made him come for no reason. He knocked on the door with his knuckles, but there was still no reply. He decided to try the doorknob. The door was open.

Frankie went through into the flat. The lights were on. The first thing he saw in the hallway was his own face reflected in a shattered mirror. There was a broken chair next to it, and a woman's shoe in a corner of the room. He went into the dining-room.

The table had been overturned, and there were the remains of plates and food all over the floor. The tablecloth had ended up on top of a standard lamp. One of the curtains had been pulled down. Bits of spaghetti with tomato sauce had stuck against one of the walls. The door to the bedroom was half open, and through it he could see a faint light.

Frankie walked slowly towards the bedroom, and after hesitating for a moment pushed the door.

Isabel lay naked across the bed.

Her face had been turned into a bloody pulp. Her lips were like aubergine-coloured spheres. Some of her hair was stuck to the pillow with blood. Her breasts looked as if they had been flattened by somebody walking across them. A tiny trickle of blood had run down one of her legs, which was hanging out of the bed, and had reached her foot. Frankie looked at her in silence, clenched his fists as if he was about to confront death, let tears run down his cheek, gave out an animal groan and dashed to the phone.

"She's not dead," said the doctor. "We'll have to notify the police."

Frankie managed to get some sleep on the bench at the police station. They'd interrogated him all night. It was five to nine in the morning. He'd been unable to convince them of his innocence. It was all turning into a long, dark nightmare. He could hear a typewriter from the inner depths of his sleep.

All he knew was that he never wanted to wake up.

A hand shook him by the shoulder.

"Hey, you," said the policeman.

Frankie shuddered and opened his eyes.

"Eh? What...?"

"You can go."

"How's Isabel?" Frankie asked.

"The chick talked before she died. It was her pimp. One Camilo Rojas. We know him. We've just pulled him in."

12

I t seemed like Frankie just couldn't stop crying.
He cried in any circumstances and for the slightest of
reasons. It was something that he simply couldn't
control.
He needed an endless supply of tissues, consumed a bottle
of eyedrops a day, and had to change his pillow-case every
morning because it was soaking wet.

If he went to buy tobacco and found the tobacconist
closed, he'd cry. If he saw a pair of cats in love, in a cartoon
film, he'd cry. If he spilt wine on his trousers, he'd cry.

The fact that Senorita Clementina had given him a small
TV set did nothing to help. Nor did the fact that Juan took
him out on his secret drinking sessions, nor the fact that
Rosita came at night to cheer him up, nor the fact that his
dose of the clap had cleared up.

When he received his second letter from Begonia
Montana, he shed several large tears, felt a couple of
tremors go through his body, and finally plucked up the
courage to read it in the privacy of his own room.

Dear Antonio,
I'd like to meet you.
    I've thought a lot about what you said in your letter,
and I think that we'll have to meet because it's going
to be impossible to nurture a relationship by letter.
    At least, that's the way I see it.
    I don't know too much about you, except what you've

told me, but you seem like a special sort of person. I can't carry on writing to you, though, unless I can meet you and see what kind of person you are.

I sometimes find that it's easier to express myself through poetry, and so I've written you a new poem, so that you can understand me better. I hope that I've succeeded, and I hope you don't mind reading it.

> Who are you, far-distant man, without a face, and
> without a look?
> What pain was it that opened your heart
> when you offered your hand?
> What will you do when, serene and disarmed,
> I walk towards your soul?

Anyway, as you know, Antonio, I live quite close to Barcelona, and I've decided to spend next weekend there.

If you want to see me, I shall be at the Canaletas fountain at eleven o'clock on Saturday morning. If you don't want to come, I say goodbye now, and wish you all the best.
Begonia.

Frankie dropped the letter onto the bed, leapt to his feet and rushed from his room.

"Senorita Clementina!" he yelled down the corridor.

"You don't have to shout, Frankie, I'm only here," she said. "Are you going to tell me what's up?"

"I've just had a letter," said Frankie, with tears in his eyes.

"So?"

"It's from the dwarf. She wants to see me on Saturday."

"I'm glad to hear it. It's about time you started going out with women again."

"But I'm scared."

"Well that's all right, Frankie. Why don't you just go and watch TV and relax for a bit."

"I don't feel like it."

"It's time for children's hour. You'll enjoy it."

"You're making fun of me, Senorita Clementina."

"You've brought this on yourself, Frankie. I've already told you, I don't want to see you crying again."

Frankie blew his nose on his handkerchief, and smiled a bit.

"Oh all right, maybe you're right..."

"Of course I'm right."

Frankie went back to his room, turned on the portable television, and took a swig at his new bottle of whiskey. He lay back on the bed and watched television for the best part of half an hour. Then he began to get bored and got up to turn it off. He crumpled the empty Ducados packet and tossed it in the air. It landed on top of the wardrobe. He went to look at himself in the mirror.

"Look here, Sinatra," he said in a low voice.

He looked into his eyes and waited for an answer.

"What?"

"You're going to have to help me."

"Help you what?"

"I want to come out on top for once in my bloody life."

"Easier said than done."

"You know what? I want to be the way I was that night in the hotel, looking out over the city, with Isabel at my side."

"Well, give it a try then."

"Do you think I can pull it off?"

"I'm not sure."

Frankie gave a disgruntled shrug.

"Me neither."

"How would it be if you rang Senora Hortensia, married her and settled for the quiet life?"

"I couldn't do it, I couldn't love her."

"What about Natalia? Maybe she's about to have your baby?"

Frankie raised his forefinger to his forehead in a disparaging gesture.

"She's crazy," he said.

"Who's the crazy one, you or her?"

"The pair of us, if you ask me."

"Look, why don't you turn on the TV and try to relax a bit?"

"I've had enough of fucking television!"

"No need to get all steamed up..."

"And on top of all that, there's the dwarf!"

"That's simple. If you don't want to go, don't go."

Frankie clicked his fingers as if things had suddenly become blindingly obvious.

"That's right," he said to himself. "If I don't want to go, I don't go."

"Hey."

"What?"

"When are you going to stop talking to yourself?"

That night, seated at his usual spot next to the key-board, in the dim light of the yellow lightbulb, staring into an ashtray full of dog-ends and with a strange smile on his face, Frankie thought about his death for the first time.

He'd get it on with Isabel when he got to heaven!

"What are you grinning at, creep?" Juan called from the doorway.

Frankie raised his eyes and his strange smile suddenly became morose.

"About dying," he answered.

"I'm not surprised — you look like death warmed up."

"That's my problem, not yours."

Juan raised one hand to his jacket pocket, took out a matchbox and tossed it casually onto the table.

"There you are," he said. "Have fun."

"With matches?"

"Look inside."

Frankie opened the matchbox and found five pink-and-black capsules inside.

"What are these?"

"Amphetamines."

"Not for me, thanks."

"They'll make you feel good, pal," Juan insisted. "You need livening up a bit. Why don't you take a couple?"

"I won't be able to sleep."

"What are you talking about, dummy?! Sleep? You're the one who's supposed to be awake all night to open the door for people."

"They'll do my head in even more than it is already."

Juan gave him a sympathetic look.

"You've got yourself into a right state..." he said, slowly.

Frankie took the whiskey and poured himself another drink.

"And I suppose if I take one of these I'll turn into the Brave Prince?"

"Well at least you'll liven up a bit."

"And what happens if I take all of them?"

"They'll send you up the wall."

Frankie took all five pills and downed them with a glass of whiskey.

A few minutes later he turned the radio up a bit, and began tapping his left foot in time with the music. His eyes were brighter than usual.

"They're not doing anything yet," he told Juan.

Then he began clicking the fingers of both hands, moving his shoulders a bit and jigging around in his seat. Finally he got up.

"You're feeling good, eh?" said Juan.

Frankie gave him a wink and went off down the corridor.

"This hotel's too scruffy. I'm going to clean it up a bit."

"Do me a favour, Frankie... It's midnight..."

Frankie returned with a bucket of water, a floorcloth, a

sponge and a broom.

"Come on, Juan, shift yourself," he ordered rapidly. "Why don't you give me a hand."

"And the cripple picked up his bed and walked!" Juan murmured.

"You'll see, we'll soon have it looking good as new," Frankie continued. "Tell you what, we could give it a lick of paint, and mend the legs of the armchair, and take a look at the plumbing."

"Slow down, chum, slow down... " said Juan, in an attempt to cool him out.

"Senorita Clementina!" Frankie shouted, hopping up and down enthusiastically, "Senorita Clementina!"

"He's taken all five," Juan thought to himself. "He's going to be speeding all night."

"Where's the hammer?" Frankie wondered out loud. "I'm sure I saw it somewhere."

In one swift movement he seized the reception armchair, turned it over, and set about examining the problem with its legs.

"Juan, why don't you give the corridor a bit of a going-over?" said Frankie. "And while you're at it, why not turn the radio up a bit?"

Senorita Clementina arrived on the scene, wrapped in a black dressing-gown and with a cigarette hanging from her lips. She was carrying Cheep-Cheep, nesting peacefully in her cleavage. She gave Frankie a baleful look.

"What on earth are you doing?" she spluttered. "You loco, or something?"

"Oh hello, Senorita Clementina — I need some nails and a pair of pincers."

"It's amphetamines," Juan explained to Senorita Clementina.

All of a sudden Frankie forgot about the armchair, took the broom and climbed on the table to get rid of a small cobweb he'd noticed in one corner of the ceiling. As he was moving across the tabletop he knocked off his whiskey glass, and it smashed on the floor.

"CAN'T A PERSON GET SOME FUCKING SLEEP?!" somebody bawled down the corridor.

The lights in people's rooms slowly flickered into life. Frankie had climbed down from the table and was pouring bleach into the water in the bucket.

"I promise you, I'll have this floor as shiny as one of those adverts on TV."

Down the corridor a number of faces loomed, ghastly grey.

"They're all drunk," said one old woman with hair like dried-up worms.

"I've got to go to work tomorrow," pleaded a small man with a face like crinkled cardboard.

"The one night when I manage to get an early night..." said a prostitute with a fag-end in her mouth.

There was a muttered expletive in Arabic.

Senorita Clementina used her imposing bulk to slow Frankie down, as she pinned him against the wall.

"*That'll do, Frankie. The party's over,*" she said, jamming her face up against his and fixing him with a steely glare.

"But I have to clean the hotel," Frankie insisted, weakly.

"If you don't stop rushing about, I'm going to kill you," she declared.

"I'm sorry..."

She thought for a moment or two, decided to let him go, and without taking her baleful eyes off him, said:

"You can do whatever you like, Frankie, but do it in SILENCE! Understand?"

"Yes, Senorita Clementina."

"Why don't you go and peel some potatoes? There's a whole sack in the kitchen, that I bought this morning."

"I'd probably end up cutting my fingers off."

"Well why don't you go for a walk, and come back when

you've calmed down a bit?"

"I'd end up running, and then they'd arrest me. It happened once before, you know, honestly..."

"What are we going to do with him?" asked Juan.

"How should I know? Tie him down in his chair... gag him... cut his tongue out..."

"Well it was your idea to give him the pills."

Senorita Clementina turned to Frankie.

"I know what would calm you down."

"What?" Frankie asked, nervously.

"A woman."

"No, please!" said Frankie, imploringly.

"There's two or three here who don't charge a lot, and if you like I'll even lend you the money."

Frankie dived for the whiskey bottle, took a large swig and sat down in his usual chair.

"I won't so much as move, all night, Senorita Clementina," he promised her.

"He'll never manage it," commented Juan. "He's going to be speeding till the morning, and then some."

"Why don't you stay down here with me, Juan?" Frankie said. "I think I'll be needing someone to talk to."

"I'm off for some shut-eye," said Juan, disappearing down the corridor.

Frankie looked anxiously at Senorita Clementina.

"Are you going away too?" he asked.

"I think I'd best not leave you on your own. You might do something daft."

"Why don't you show me your photo albums with the film stars? I'd like to see them."

"Now that's not a bad idea. I'll bring them right away."

Left on his own, Frankie got up and started pacing up and down the reception area. Then a strong impulse made him open the door and rush down the stairs to the street, two steps at a time. He took a rapid look up and down both sides of Calle Hospital, picked up the empty dustbin and ran back up the stairs.

Senorita Clementina was waiting for him with two photo albums on her knee, a bottle of muscatel at her side, and Cheep-Cheep tucked into her cleavage.

"Have you any photos of Sinatra?" Frankie asked.

"Sure. Several."

"You won't mind if I look at them standing up, will you, so that I can move around a bit?"

"Go ahead."

Senorita Clementina opened one of the albums with a ceremonial flourish, and one by one turned the pages for a very restless Frankie.

"I love them all," she said fondly. "They've helped me a lot, you know."

Frankie thought of the club's brochure, with its little photographs of each member. This album was different.

Platinum blondes coming down the marble staircases of sumptuous mansions. Famous actors smiling from the driving seats of sports cars. There they were, at glittering parties surrounded by photographers. Or on white yachts gliding over azure seas. They were winning Oscars... feted... distant...

"There he is," said Senorita Clementina.

There he was. Sinatra. It was a picture of one of his many weddings. His wife was small and pretty, with a face that was a bit boney and with blonde hair that had been cut a bit too short. She looked about thirty years younger than her husband. She was carrying a small bouquet of flowers in one hand. He was holding her round the waist and she was kissing him on the cheek. Both of them were smiling. They looked happy.

Frankie looked at the photograph for a long while. Then he looked away, gave a little kick to the rubbish bin which he'd left in the middle of reception, lit a Ducados and stood there with the lighted match a couple of inches from his face.

Senorita Clementina gave him a worried look and asked: "Why don't you say what's on your mind?"

Frankie flicked out the match and answered:

"I'm thinking about how I'm never going to see Isabel again."

13

It was a lousy Saturday morning. A dirty rain was falling over the city. Steely blue flashes of lightning carved through the heavy skies, which dissolved into cold drops of rain. Water and scurrying rats ran down the gutters. Traffic had stopped. Far away a sound of sirens indicated flooded basements. The posters outside the bars were flapping in a murderous wind.

There was nobody on the Ramblas.

The only person to be seen was a lone figure sitting on one of the benches near to the Canaletas fountain. A man, wearing a cheap transparent plastic raincoat. He had his hands in his pockets, his legs stretched out, an unlit cigarette in his mouth, and his gaze lost on some distant point.

It was Frankie.

He waited calmly. As if he no longer had anything to lose, and it made no odds to him whether he was sitting here or somewhere else. The wry smile had returned to his lips. He didn't even feel the raindrops running down his face.

Another figure, small and indistinct, began to take shape as it came out of the entrance to the metro. It bobbed along in the pouring rain. It seemed to be carrying an enormous umbrella, and was wearing a white headscarf. It was a girl. The barrel-shaped figure came up to Frankie. When she was at his side she gave him a smile in the form of a grimace, stretched out a podgy hand, and said:

"Hello, Antonio. I'm Begonia Montana."

Frankie stood up and shook her hand. He was too confused to say anything. He managed a smile and Begonia rubbed her nose with her forefinger.

"Do you want to come under the umbrella?" she asked.

"No, I'm fine," said Frankie after a while.

"Shall we go for a drink?"

"Yes, sure."

They wandered down the Ramblas towards the sea. Side by side. In silence. Every now and then they looked at each other and smiled weakly. Begonia Montana found it an effort to keep up with Frankie. She struggled to keep pace with him. She seemed to bounce along, somehow. Frankie looked down to his right, saw that she couldn't keep up with him, and slowed down.

She was puffing a bit.

"Thanks, Antonio. I was getting worn out."

They entered a frankfurter bar on San Pablo, and took one of the few tables in the place. Frankie shed his raincoat and began drying his hair with a paper serviette. Begonia Montana put her bag on the table, glanced momentarily in one of the mirrors, and then sat down in reverent silence.

"What would you like to drink?"

"A coffee."

"I fancy a brandy, myself."

"OK."

Begonia Montana shifted in her seat. She seemed to have problems getting her elbows onto the table. She settled herself more comfortably and finally found a good position. Frankie offered her a Ducados and she shook her head and chewed on a fingernail.

"I'm not a very talkative sort, you know," said Frankie.

"Me neither," answered Begonia.

Frankie was beginning to feel uncomfortable. He couldn't sit there for much longer without saying something. Maybe the brandy would help him find the words. He called the waiter and ordered another. Begonia Montana started playing with a toothpick. She was avoiding his eyes, too.

"It's stopped raining," Frankie commented, turning his head to the street.

"Don't you like rain?"

"So so."

Frankie downed his second cognac. By now, Begonia Montana had broken three toothpicks.

"Listen, Antonio..."

"Yes?"

"Would you like me to go away?"

At that moment Frankie looked her in the eye. Her eyes were blue and yellow. They seemed too large in relation to the rest of her face. One of them was slightly higher than the other. They moved gently. They seemed to expect nothing. They had a look of kindness.

"No, don't go away," Frankie answered, and, almost without realizing it, he took her hand.

Begonia Montana showed no surprise. She had been studying Frankie's eyes.

"I'm happy to be your friend," she said, smiling, and moving her fat little fingers in Frankie's damp hand.

"Would you like another coffee, Begonia?"

"Yes. With a dash of milk. Just for a change."

"OK. What do you think, shall we go for a walk afterwards?"

"I'd love to."

"Do you know the Boqueriá market?"

"No."

"It's very near here. I usually go there very early. When I finish work, I like just wandering round and looking at everything."

"It must be fun."

"Do you know something, Begonia?"

"What?"

"I like being with you. A lot."

Begonia Montana raised her eyebrows, opened her mouth, and momentarily stuck out her tongue.

"Nobody's ever said that to me before," she replied.

"Is that why you joined the club?"

"I suppose we all need someone, really."

"But people get close to each other, and then they disappear. Some of them die, some of them go crazy, and some of them turn into something else."

"Not me."

Frankie stared at the bottom of his empty brandy glass.

"Look, Begonia, I'm not going to tell you about my life. It's all in the past, now. Let sleeping dogs lie."

"Do you like strawberries?" she asked, out of the blue.

"Sure," replied Frankie, surprised.

"We could go to the market and buy some strawberries. What do you think?"

"Fine."

"I'm sure it'll make you feel better."

"As long as you stay with me..."

"Sure, silly."

Begonia Montana and Frankie wandered among the people that were moving around in the enormous market. They paused to look at strange shellfish, the silvery lustre of big fishes, the strong colour of dead meat, the mounds of cheeses, the gentle hills of fruit...

"Begonia, there's a bar over there. Let's go and sit down."

It was just a little bar, with three or four stools, set into one wall of the market. It was enjoyable sitting there, drinking something and letting luck take care of the rest.

"Seems to me that you can't live without bars, Antonio."

"The thing is, they look after me, you see."

Frankie resolved Begonia Montana's difficulties with the stool. He took her by the waist and sat her gently on it. She seemed happy sitting up there, looking at the sights of the market.

"I'm now going to drink the first beer of my life," she declared enthusiastically.

"Haven't you ever drunk alcohol before?"

"Never."

"Two beers, please," Frankie called.

Begonia Montana looked at the cool yellow liquid and the white froth on top of it, and gave a little chink of her glass against Frankie's.

"Cheers, Antonio."

"Cheers, Begonia."

They drank for two hours on end. They began talking about the things that really interested them. She leaned back slightly over the bar, and rested her head on one hand. Frankie remembered what Contreras had told him. And it was still only three in the afternoon.

"Do you know where people go when they die?" Frankie asked.

Begonia Montana pointed at the roof of the market with one finger.

"They go up there, flying."

"How do you know?"

"I dreamt about it."

"Isabel must be flying, then," he said to himself. He smiled, and then asked:

"And what about when people go crazy?"

"They stay where they are, but somewhere else."

Frankie looked at her uncomprehendingly.

"You know a lot of things."

"It must be the beer."

"Why don't you write something, Begonia? You could write on the serviette."

"What, now?"

"Sure."

She opened her handbag, took out a blue biro, chewed on the end of it, and thought for a moment. Then she began to write. When she had finished, she folded the serviette neatly into four equal parts and handed it to Frankie.

"There you are," she said simply.

Frankie unfolded the serviette and read:

I WANT TO KNOW WHAT IT'S LIKE TO GO WITH A MAN.

"Shall we have another beer, Begonia?" was all that he could say.

"I'll fall over."

"Are you feeling bad?"

"A bit."

"You should eat something."

"I don't feel like it. Maybe we'd best go out and get some air."

"OK."

Begonia Montana and Frankie left the market and walked over to sit on one of the benches in Plaza San Agustin. Next to them, three or four drunks were passing a bottle of wine among themselves, and looked at them without interest. The sun managed to break through every now and then, between heavy clouds that were being driven along by the wind. Pigeons were eating bits of bread that a lone woman was putting down for them. A tranquil scene.

She leaned her head back, closed her eyes, and rested her hand on Frankie's tense thigh.

"You still haven't said anything, Antonio."

"About what?"

"About what I wrote on the serviette."

Frankie felt the alcohol warming up his brain. He was on the point of breaking into a run, or maybe answering Begonia Montana with something brutal. He looked at her. Her little body was perched serenely on the bench.

"Have you never been with a man, then?" he asked, in a hoarse voice.

"I told you in the letter. Never."

"And you want to know what it's like..."

"Just once."

"I thought you got your pleasure in your poems."

Begonia Montana opened her eyes and looked at him searchingly.

"Haven't you realized yet that I'm a woman?"

Frankie bowed his head and covered his face with his hands. What he needed now was a drink.

"We could buy a bottle and go home and watch TV," he said at last, rising to his feet.

"Thank you, Antonio," Begonia replied.

Manolo opened the hotel door to them.

He more or less ignored Frankie, but his eyes were immediately drawn to the presence of Begonia Montana. He didn't say anything, or do anything. He just stood there looking.

Frankie staggered a bit. Then, with the same hand that was carrying the bottle of brandy he had just opened, he pushed Manolo to one side and entered reception. She followed, rather unsure of herself.

"Frankie... " Manolo murmured.

"What's up?"

"No... nothing."

"Where's Senorita Clementina?"

"She's gone to the pictures with Juan."

Frankie looked irritated and took another swig at the bottle.

"I wanted to have a talk with her for a moment," he said to himself. Then, abruptly, he turned to Begonia Montana.

"Shall we go?" he asked, from the start of the dark passageway. They entered his room.

Begonia Montana looked into Frankie's troubled eyes and walked towards him. Frankie locked the door and turned on the portable television. The bed was unmade, and the odd sock was lying on the floor. She kicked off her shoes, lay on the bed, rested her head on the pillow and examined her surroundings.

"My head's spinning, Antonio," she said, in a far-away voice.

"Shall I make you a coffee?"

"No, stay here."

Frankie sat on the edge of the bed with his back to Begonia Montana. The only light on them was the flickering grey of the television, which neither of them was watching.

"Antonio..."

Frankie turned round slowly and looked at her over his shoulder.

"What?"

"Do you think you'll be able to do it?"

"I don't know."

"Me neither."

An expression began to appear on Frankie's face. The look of a man who is about to walk a high wire strung between two skyscrapers. He launched a further onslaught on the brandy bottle. He gave a sombre wink to the damp towel that was hanging from the washbasin, and once again turned to Begonia Montana.

"Well, I think I'm ready," he declared.

She didn't move.

"This is crazy," she said, after a few moments.

"So?" Frankie answered defiantly.

Begonia Montana had begun to tremble slightly.

"Why don't you turn off the TV, Antonio?"

"Because I want to see you with no clothes on."

She sat up a bit on the bed. Her face was pale. She looked at his body. She realized that she was seeing double.

"Really?" she asked.

"Sure," Frankie answered, in a voice made hoarse by the brandy.

Begonia Montana rolled over on the bed and gradually

snuggled her body up to Frankie's. She could smell his fragrance of black tobacco and alcohol. Her head seemed to be flying all around the room. He, on the other hand, was waiting, resolutely. And then it happened.

Just as her moist lips were about to touch Frankie's for the first time, a liquid earthquake shook her stomach, rose irresistibly up her throat, and exploded in a vile jet that splattered across the unmade bed in which she would now never find love.

14

Rosita was serving a beer from behind the bar. She was wearing her blonde wig again. She had a black eye, and one of her cheekbones was slightly swollen. She appeared to be absorbed in her work.

Frankie came into the bar, looked over at her, paused to light a cigarette and then went to the counter. It was almost midnight. Senorita Clementina had given him the night off.

"Antonio, darling!" Rosita exclaimed when she saw him. She adjusted her wig with the palm of her hand, and gave him a couple of kisses. One on each cheek. Frankie couldn't even raise a smile.

"Give me something strong," he said.

"Mother of God, what's the matter with you?" said Rosita, rolling her eyes in alarm.

Frankie was looking a lot worse than the first time they'd met. He was on tranquillizers, and he hadn't been shaving either.

"Nothing. I'm just done for," he answered.

"But angel, you can't go round the place with a face like that. I'm going to make you up a little something that will do you good."

"OK," said Frankie, gazing into the street.

Rosita served him a small glass of casala with raisins.

"Drink that, honey. It'll bring some colour to your cheeks. You're not looking yourself, poor thing..."

Frankie downed the casala in one gulp.

"Have another one, angel," said Rosita, and she refilled his glass.

Frankie took one of the raisins, put it in his mouth and chewed it absent-mindedly. Then he looked at Rosita and inquired casually and with no particular interest:

"What happened to your face?"

"I didn't tell you, honey. You see, Ramon is back. We're living together now. I'm so happy, Antonio..."

"And... ?"

"Ramon is a nervous sort, you know. Sometimes he gets annoyed with me over the silliest things, but he's so goodhearted, and he's ever so goodlooking..."

"Sure."

Rosita looked at her watch and then at the two or three customers finishing their drinks in the bar.

"I'm going to lock up, darling," she said. "So's we can spend a bit of time together here, just you and me... have a few drinks. If you like, you can come with me afterwards, when I go cigarette-selling in Plaza Real."

"Are you a cigarette seller now?"

"Yes. You see, since I'm back with Ramon I need the money. All he eats is prime steak..."

"Jesus!"

When the last customer had left, Rosita locked the bar door, put a couple of coins in the juke box and sat down at the table with Frankie.

"Haven't you found yourself another lovely lady, Antonio?" she asked, with a look of concern.

"I'm never touching another woman as long as I live."

"You're just going through a bad patch..."

"I talked with Natalia yesterday. You know the one I mean?"

"The girl who wanted to have your baby."

"That's right. She rang me. It sounded as if she was having trouble speaking, like her tongue had gone to sleep, or something. First she said she was in Paris buying hats, then that she was talking to me from a phone box in Hospitalet, and then that she never wanted to see me again because I'd steal her baby and sell it to the gypsies."

"For God's sake, honey, the kid's in a bad way..."

Frankie couldn't think of anything else to say. He sat there, motionless and vacant, until Rosita switched off the bar lights, ushered him out into the street, and then walked him back to the hotel door.

"I'm off now, angel. Look after yourself," Rosita told him, giving him another kiss and heading off down to the Ramblas, with a carrier-bag full of packs of imported cigarettes, and singing a love song to herself.

When Frankie returned, he saw Senorita Clementina in deep conversation with an empty bottle of muscatel. She was sitting in his chair, with no shoes and with her dressing-gown half open.

Frankie felt like he was waking from a bad dream.

"Are you all right, Senorita Clementina?" he asked, cautiously.

She turned her head and gave him a surprised look.

"Sure. Why?"

"I thought that..."

" ...that I was talking to myself?"

"Well, yes..." said Frankie, confused.

"I don't see what's so odd about that. I've heard you doing it..."

"Maybe."

"Did you know that Juan has gone?"

"Gone?" asked Frankie, incredulously.

"He's robbed me of forty thousand pesetas and gone missing. I was just celebrating. Do you fancy a drink?"

"Yes, please."

"He was getting on my nerves anyway. He'd never take a shower, see. He said that's what he was used to in prison. He had a very odd smell, a bit like a monkey, you know."

At that moment the doorbell rang.

Frankie opened the door and saw a little bald-headed man wearing round glasses and a timid smile. He had a grey mac and carried an old battered suitcase in his hand.

"Good evening. I was wondering if you had a room..."

"Come in," Frankie replied, as he ushered him into reception.

Senorita Clementina closed her dressing-gown and tucked the muscatel behind her chair. The little man gave her a quick glance and then turned to Frankie.

"What's your cheapest room?"

"Three hundred pesetas."

"Could I see it?"

"Sure."

Frankie took one of the keys from the board and set off down the corridor.

"Follow me, please."

The little man put his case down and followed Frankie. Senorita Clementina stayed behind to take another swig at the muscatel. Frankie was not long in returning, still followed by the little man. He sat down at his desk, opened the guest register and began to write.

He was just about to take the little man's money and hand him his key when he noticed a gun pointed straight at his head.

"Don't move," he said. "I am Brother Blanco Sol."

Senorita Clementina moved to rise from her seat. The little man turned towards her.

"You... come here," he ordered.

"This is my hotel, and I'll do what I like," she replied, defiantly.

"I've got a gun, though. Right, now we'll all go to the room!"

Senorita Clementina and Frankie moved cautiously towards the corridor. The little man picked up his case, and without taking his eyes off them followed them down to the room.

"Sit down on the bed," he ordered, as he shut the door and leaned up against it.

"All right, Brother Antonio. Talk!"

Frankie looked at him uncomprehendingly.

"What do you want me to say?"

"Relax, Frankie," said Senorita Clementina.

"I want to know how you have managed to become the Wicked One and why you have not repented."

"I've not done anything."

"Well, you're going to have to do something now."

Brother Blanco Sol opened his suitcase, and, still watching them intently, took out a long white tunic, a crucifix, two little candles, various pictures of saints, a pair of rosaries, a bottle of water and a bible.

"Put on the tunic, Brother Antonio," said the little man, throwing it across to him.

"Do what he says," Senorita Clementina whispered. "I'll try and get his gun."

Brother Blanco Sol then began sprinkling holy water in every corner of the room — still keeping a firm grip on his gun.

"There you are," said Frankie, once he'd put the tunic on.

"Kneel down and start praying."

"At this precise moment I can't remember any prayers... honestly."

"That's another proof that you are the Wicked One. I should kill you right now," said Blanco Sol, lighting the candles and still not taking his eyes off Frankie.

"You're wrong," Senorita Clementina interrupted. "I am the Wicked One. If you give us the time, I shall tell you how this came to be."

"You're lying!"

"Listen, sir, please... " said Frankie, desperately. "I'm not the Wicked One or anything like that. Why don't you just leave us in peace and take your things and go?"

The crucifix suddenly loomed above him.

"You can't fool Him!"

"What are we going to do, Senorita Clementina?" Frankie asked, in a trembling voice.

"Keep calm and wait."

Brother Blanco Sol put down the crucifix and drank a little of the holy water from his bottle. Then, addressing himself to the heavens, he began to speak:

"The moment has arrived. Once and for all, the Wicked One will be defeated and divine goodness will reign in the world. Finally I have completed my mission, and..."

"Excuse me, can I go to the toilet?" asked Clementina.

"No!"

"But I'm about to wet myself. What am I supposed to do?"

"Hold on to it!"

"Impossible. I'll just have to do it right here," said Senorita Clementina. She stood up, shed her dressing-gown and stood there, completely naked.

Brother Blanco Sol's expression slowly changed as this colossal female body appeared before his eyes. His breathing became agitated, and the hand that was holding the gun wavered. His lips moved slightly, as if he was trying to say something, and an unexpected tear spilled down his cheek. Overwhelmed, he dropped his gun, went down on his knees and exclaimed:

"Lord! It's a holy woman!"

Senorita Clementina, without losing her poise for a moment, took his gun and put her dressing-gown back on. She lit a cigarette, winked at Frankie and helped him to raise Brother Blanco Sol to his feet.

"Poor man, looks like he needs a drink," she said, with an air of concern. "Come on Frankie, let's all go to reception and have a drink."

"Aren't you going to call the police?" asked Frankie, still shaking.

"The police? Why?"

"This man was trying to kill me."

"Well he wouldn't hurt a fly now..."

"Yes, but..."

"Don't worry Frankie. The only thing that's happened to this man is that for the first time in his life he's seen a woman with no clothes on. That's all."

Brother Blanco Sol was sitting on the edge of the bed, crying.

"Please, don't hurt me. I love everybody in the world, I've always tried to help people..."

"With a gun?!" Frankie interrupted him.

"I just wanted to stop the Holy Mother from crying."

"The best thing would be if *you* stopped crying. You're going to wake everyone in the hotel," said Senorita Clementina. "Let's get out of here."

"Agreed," said Frankie. "I could use a drink too. I'm not feeling too bright."

"Don't forget to take the cassock off, Frankie. It doesn't really suit you..."

The three of them sat down to drink muscatel. Brother Blanco Sol's hands were trembling as he downed his wine.

"Could I have a bit more?" he said.

"Sure. Now, what's this all about? I presume you don't normally go around doing this sort of thing..."

"No... you won't tell my mother, though, will you?"

"No."

"And not the Virgin Mary either?"

"Her neither."

Frankie sat and drank in silence. He was pale and looking worried.

"I joined the club because my mother left me," said Brother Blanco Sol.

"I see," said Senorita Clementina, as she busied herself emptying bullets from the gun.

"She left me. She went off with a man. Now I live on

my own, and I have to do my own cooking, but I can't cook..."

"And that's why you go round with this gun?"

"Well, I wanted to do away with the Wicked One."

"Fine, fine," said Frankie, in a tired voice.

"You say your mother left you for another man?" Senorita Clementina asked, confused.

"That's right. She died, and went off to live with the Wicked One."

"Carry on, please."

"I started writing to everyone in the club, but I didn't get even one answer. I needed my mother, or some other woman, to look after me. That was why I started talking to the Virgin Mary. And then I found that she loved me. But very often she used to cry, because the Wicked One was after her, trying to kill her."

"And how did you decide that Frankie, I mean Antonio, was the Wicked One?"

"She told me so."

"Who?"

"The Virgin Mary."

"'What are we going to do with him, Frankie?" Senorita Clementina asked, after a brief pause.

"I don't know. You decide."

Senorita Clementina lit a cigarette, smoked it in silence for a minute or two, and finally shook her head slowly and said:

"All right then, you can go."

As a shamefaced and silent Brother Blanco Sol left the dimly-lit reception area, Senorita Clementina turned to Frankie and gave him a long look.

"Do you need anything?" she asked.

"I'm not feeling very well. I think he was the last straw."

"I told you not to take so many tranquillizers, Frankie."

"I'm scared, Senorita Clementina."

She understood everything. She went back to sit in her

chair, took a drink from the bottle, and then, sweet as her own muscatel, she told him:

"Come over here, Frankie."

Like an exhausted traveller just about to reach his destination, Frankie came over to her, sat on the floor next to her chair, and rested his head on her thighs.

She stroked his hair slowly and gently.

"You really deserve someone to love you," she said softly.

Frankie abandoned himself to the warmth of Senorita Clementina. He shut his eyes and began to see a strange and unaccustomed light approaching him, like the dawn.

"You should have a shave, Frankie," she said as she ran her fingers over his cold, rough cheeks.

"I will, I will," Frankie promised, as if from a distance.

"And are you going to stop taking tranquillizers?"

Frankie couldn't answer.

Senorita Clementina sat up slowly, opened the front of her dressing-gown, rested his head between her warm breasts and told him in a low voice:

"Take it easy, Frankie. Take it easy..."

The finest contemporary Spanish and Latin American writing . . .

. . . published by

SERPENT'S
TAIL

Daniel Moyano
THE DEVIL'S TRILL

'The first English publication, in superb translation, of one of Argentina's finest writers (in exile). Moyano, like his hero Triclinio, finds harmonies in discord and, playing ironic acompaniment to the Devil's tunes, brings music out of madness.... With fine wit and artistry, Moyano has written a political parable that movingly sings the triumph of the human spirit.'

SUNDAY TIMES

'Daniel Moyano is a superb writer.... The absence of an English translation of his writing is one of those literary lapses one reads about as happening to other places and other ages.'

ANDREW GRAHAM-YOOLL

'An eloquent defence of artistic integrity and freedom . . . the book is a real triumph.'

JOHN KING

'Daniel Moyano's deep realism blends both modern and classical prose, progressive thought and a profound faith in the ability of human beings to suvive.'

RAFAEL CONTE

120 pages £6.50 (paper)

Juan Goytisolo
LANDSCAPES AFTER THE BATTLE

'Juan Goytisolo is one of the most rigorous and original contemporary writers. His books are a strange mixture of pitiless autobiography, the debunking of mythologies and conformist fetishes, passionate exploration of the periphery of the West – in particular of the Arab world which he knows intimately – and audacious linguistic experiment. All these qualities feature in *Lanscapes After the Battle*, an unsettling, apocalyptic work, splendidly translated by Helen Lane.'   MARIO VARGAS LLOSA

'*Landscapes After the Battle* . . . a cratered terrain littered with obscenities and linguistic violence, an assault on "good taste" and the reader's notions of what a novel should be.'

THE OBSERVER

'Fierce, highly unpleasant and very funny.'

THE GUARDIAN

'A short, exhilarating tour of the emergence of pop culture, sexual liberation and ethnic militancy.'

NEW STATESMAN

'Helen Lane's rendering reads beautifully, capturing the whimsicality and rhythms of the Spanish without sacrificing accuracy, but rightly branching out where literal translation simply does not work.'

TIMES LITERARY SUPPLEMENT

176 pages £7.95 (paper)

Juan Goytisolo
MARKS OF IDENTITY

Marks of Identity is the first volume of Goytisolo's major trilogy. The other two books, *Count Julian* and *Juan the Landless*, are also to be published by Serpent's Tail.

'For me *Marks of Identity* was my first novel. It was forbidden publication in Spain. For twelve years after that everything I wrote was forbidden in Spain. So I realized that my decision to attack the Spanish language through its culture was correct. But what was most important for me was that I no longer exercised censorship on myself, I was free writer. This search for and conquest of freedom was the most important thing to me.'

Juan Goytisolo, in an interview with CITY LIMITS

'Juan Goytisolo is by some distance the most important living novelist from Spain . . . and *Marks of Identity* is undoubtedly his most important novel, some would say the most significant work by a Spanish writer since 1939, a truly historic milestone.'

THE GUARDIAN

'A masterpiece which should whet the appetites of British readers for the rest of the trilogy.'

TIMES LITERARY SUPPLEMENT

352 pages £8.95 (paper)

Jorge Amado
DONA FLOR AND HER TWO HUSBANDS

Dona Flor's first husband, a notorious gambler and womanizer, has unexpectedly died. When the local pharmacist proposes to her, she accepts his hand in marriage. However, he is unable to satisfy her erotic visions. Then one night her first husband materializes at the foot of her bed . . .

'Jorge Amado has been writing immensely popular novels for fifty years. His books are on the grand scale, long, lavish, highly coloured, exuberant. . . . Amado has vigour, panache, raciness . . . a reputation as a master storyteller.'   TLS

'a bacchanalia of a book: a veritable orgy of sex, food, gambling and mayhem'   CITY LIMITS

576 pages £7.95 (paper)

Luisa Valenzuela
THE LIZARD'S TAIL

'Luisa Valenzuela has written a wonderfully free ingenious novel about sensuality and power and death, the "I" and literature. Only a Latin American could have written *The Lizard's Tail*, but there is nothing like it in contemporary Latin American literature.'   SUSAN SONTAG

'By knotting together the writer's and the subject's fates, Valenzuela creates an extraordinary novel whose thematic ferocity and baroque images explore a political situation too exotically appalling for reportage.'   THE OBSERVER

'Its exotic, erotic forces seduce with consummate, subliminal force.'   BLITZ

'Don't classify it as another wonder of "magic realism": read, learn and fear.'   TIME OUT

'*The Lizard's Tail* will probably sell far fewer copies than Isabel Allende's inferior *Of Love and Shadows*, and that is a great pity. [It] is a wild adventurous book . . . a gripping and challenging read.'
                                         THIRD WORLD QUARTERLY

288 pages £7.95 (paper)